She got lucky

"It was dangerous to do what you did, Holly Nichols," David stated softly.

Confused, Holly leaned against the counter and mentally cataloged everything they'd done that evening. "What was dangerous about going to McDonald's and an arcade?"

"I'm talking about that ad you ran." He moved slowly toward her, an unreadable expression on his face. "You don't know anything about me, Holly. For all you know I could be some kind of pervert."

Her heart leaped into her throat as he halted a few inches from her. Placing a hand on either side of her, he trapped her against the counter.

"Are . . . are you?" she whispered huskily, captivated by his smoky jade-green eyes. She felt no fear, only a swift hot longing to be in his arms.

"No," he admitted softly, then shrugged, his eyes gleaming with a devilish light. "What I'm feeling now is perfectly normal. . . ."

Phyllis Roberts wrote *A Man Like David* in three and a half weeks—the first time. Five years and numerous rewrites later she ventured to enter the finished product in the Romance Writers of America Golden Heart contest. She became a finalist, and the rest, as they say, is history.

She's now juggling the demands of being a published author with her duties as a legal secretary and the rigors facing a single mother of three. But the love and support of her colleagues help ease the load considerably. And hearing her children say, "We're proud of you, Mom" makes it all worthwhile.

A Man Like David

PHYLLIS ROBERTS

Harlequin Books

TORONTO • NEW YORK • LONDON
AMSTERDAM • PARIS • SYDNEY • HAMBURG
STOCKHOLM • ATHENS • TOKYO • MILAN

To Diane,
who was the first to tell me
I could do this and who stayed around
to make sure I did.
And to Dan and Colleen,
my own Nebraska Valentines.

Published August 1988

ISBN 0-373-25313-3

1

"CAN SHE REALLY do this, John?"

The attorney noted the brooding frown on D. W. Branson's face and slowly nodded his head. "She can file anything she wants, Bran," he said, choosing his words with care, "but whether the court will issue an injunction in this matter is questionable."

"Damn!" Flinging the letter down on his desk, Branson abruptly stood and strode to the window. "How did this situation get so out of hand," he muttered, staring moodily at the Indianapolis skyline. He had neither the time nor the inclination to get tangled up in a lawsuit. Running his hand through dark hair that had grown so long it brushed his collar, he grimaced. Hell, he didn't even have time to get a haircut.

John Hanover's brow wrinkled in worry. He was obviously concerned for the troubled man he silently observed across the room from him, a man he had called his friend for nearly fifteen years. The effects of the pressure and stress Bran was under were beginning to show. He rarely laughed anymore. The lines in his lean face had deepened over the past year and strands of gray streaked the black hair above his ears.

"What you need is a vacation," John said in a tone that suggested he knew he was wasting his time. Bran hadn't slowed down long enough to take a vacation in all the time they'd known each other.

Moving away from the window, Bran began to pace restlessly about the room, his hands thrust into the pockets of his tailored slacks. This restlessness, along with a strong sense of something missing in his life, had been building steadily over the past year.

It isn't a vacation I need, he thought, *it's a woman.* Not one who was angry enough to threaten him with a court injunction, but a warm, willing woman. The right woman might be just what he needed to ease this nagging restlessness that had begun about the same time he had realized he was heartily sick of relationships without commitment. Those affairs had left him with an even deeper sense of loneliness when they were over. But perhaps he was carrying this self-enforced celibacy too far. It wasn't difficult to find a willing female, but the kind of woman he wanted—needed—was much more elusive.

Returning to the massive oak desk, Bran sat down and reached for the letter again. Typed on pale gray stationery with the elegant burgundy letterhead of the H. C. Nichols Agency, Chartered Life Underwriter, it told Mr. D. W. Branson, in no uncertain terms, that he was making a serious error.

She had a way with words, he thought, knowing damn well the lady was telling him he was a first-class bastard.

"Well, do you have any suggestions about how I might get my butt out of this sling?" he asked John with a rueful grin.

"Have you tried talking to her?"

Bran shook his head regretfully. "No, and that's my own fault. This is the third letter I've received from her and I never answered the other two. She has every right to be angry."

John arched a brow in surprise. "That isn't like you. What's going on, Bran?"

Frowning in self-reproach, Branson felt a rush of gratitude for the lack of censure in the other man's voice. "What kind of reason can I offer, John? That I've been so wrapped up in the civic center construction problems that I just haven't had the time? That isn't a reason, it's an excuse. Those people don't care about a project that's being built thirty miles away. They're worried about their office building being torn down." He leaned back in his chair and let out a long sigh. "There are times when I almost wish I could be someone else."

Reaching into the pocket of his gray suit coat, John removed a pipe and a packet of tobacco. After filling the bowl and lighting it, he looked up at Bran, his blue eyes pensive. "The building has to come down. You know it and those tenants know it."

"They know it all right, but they didn't hear it from me. I really screwed up," Bran admitted with frustration. "I should have called a meeting with them weeks ago, when I first realized it would be more economical to replace it than to renovate it. I wanted to wait until I had an alternative plan to offer them while the new building is being erected, but it didn't quite work out that way. Word leaked out before I got all the loose ends tied up. Now the meeting is scheduled and I'm not sure where I stand. I'll be walking into a room full of hostile people, with a mountain of points against me. You know I don't like working with that kind of odds."

The attorney's wide mouth curved in a wry grin; D. W. Branson was accustomed to having the cards stacked in his favor. Pointing the stem of the pipe at the letter, he said, "Talk to her, Bran. Make the time somehow and talk to her before that meeting next week. She seems to be their unofficial leader. If you can sway her to your way of thinking, explain the reasons behind your decision to raze the building, you'll be in a better position with the rest of the tenants. Or, if you want, I'll go talk to her."

Branson shook his head. "No, I can't let you do my dirty work for me. I'll have my secretary call and set up an appointment. Maybe I can get out of this thing with my hide intact or, at the very least, with just a few minor scars."

"If it's any consolation, you may have strong grounds for a lawsuit yourself. The weaknesses in that building should have shown up long before you purchased it, not after you had already begun restoration work. I've ordered an investigation of the engineering firm that did the preliminary report. It was the first time we used that particular firm and they may end up our prime target if it comes to a court case. We would have to prove that the sellers knew how badly the structure had weakened and withheld the information. The courts frown on lack of disclosure of that magnitude."

Branson heard what John was saying, knowing that he would do whatever was necessary to get to the bottom of this disaster, but his thoughts were dominated by the H. C. Nichols Agency and the fire-breathing woman who ran it. "John, just what does a Chartered Life Underwriter do?"

"Estate planning, tailoring business and life insurance packages to fit a client's special needs, that sort of thing."

Branson shuddered as a depressing image of Ms. H. C. Nichols rose in his mind. In his imagination, she bore a startling resemblance to his tenth-grade English teacher, with wire-rimmed glasses perched on her long nose, hair pulled back in a prim bun, and a plump, fortyish figure clad in a severely tailored suit.

Later, after John left, Branson sat alone in his office, silently berating himself for allowing this situation to get out of hand. He hated losing control of any problem, especially when it could have been easily avoided. A simple phone call. A letter. Now he felt compelled to meet with the furious Ms. Nichols face-to-face.

Picking up the telephone, he punched the intercom button and flashed a rare, devilish grin that was seen by no one. "I'll bet the lady has the sense of humor of an undertaker," he muttered to himself.

HOLLY NICHOLS had to laugh. A little voice deep inside her insisted this was no laughing matter, but she couldn't help it. Alone in her office, with no one to witness her mirth, she laughed until her sides ached and tears blurred her vision. This day had been one for the books.

The telephone rang and Holly clamped her lips together to contain her laughter. She would have to regain some control if she hoped to answer the phone with any semblance of professionalism. By the third ring, by sheer will, she had that control.

"Hi, Holly. How's the search for a fiancé going?"

At the sound of her secretary's voice, Holly felt the laughter bubbling up again and fought to suppress it. "You picked a fine day to be sick, Susan Martin! I should have you charged with desertion. If what I've seen today is any indication of what's available, heaven help the single, female population of Indianapolis!"

"That bad, huh?"

"Worse! And to top it all off, that temporary the agency sent was a total airhead. Honestly, Susan, I've used temporaries before and I probably will again, but this one didn't have the brain of a sand flea. She has the appointment calendar so messed up I doubt if even you can straighten it out."

Susan gave a hoot of laughter. "Well, Holly, you'll have to admit the poor girl got an interesting introduction to the world of a chartered life underwriter. Not everyone advertises in the paper for a fiancé for the weekend, not to mention dragging him off to Valentine, Nebraska!"

Holly frowned at the voice coming out of the phone. "You don't sound sick. Are you sure you didn't just cop out on me?"

"Honest, Holly," Susan exclaimed. "I must have picked up some lousy twenty-four-hour virus, but I am feeling better now and I'll be back to work tomorrow. Do you have any more interviews scheduled or have you exhausted the possibilities?"

Holly gave a long sigh. "There's one more, and he should be here any minute. I don't know how I let that crazy sister of mine talk me into this. I would never have gone through with it if she hadn't dared me. You know I could never resist a dare. We may have to find another way to get even with Michael James Nichols."

"Maybe you'll get lucky and Don Johnson will wander in with a free weekend on his hands."

"The way my luck has run so far, it would more than likely be Don Rickles."

"I hate to change the subject, but did Mr. Branson show up for his appointment?"

Holly's expression changed to one of disgust. "The snake canceled! I knew it was too good to be true when you told me he wanted to see me. Big shots like him don't have the time to be concerned about a small business like mine." Though Holly had never met D. W. Branson, or even seen a picture of him, she'd heard and read various things about him over the years. Not all were flattering. Her eyes narrowed. "If he really cared, he would have contacted me long before this. He didn't even bother to acknowledge my existence until I threatened him with a court injunction."

"The other tenants were just as upset as you. No one liked the idea of uprooting their business and relocating."

"It wasn't just that, though," Holly interjected. "Many of us chose to locate our businesses here in the first place because this building has a lot of character. I know it sounds silly in this age of microchips and microwaves, but twelve-foot ceilings, wainscoting and stained glass still hold a certain appeal." She failed to mention an antiquated elevator that worked *most* of the time and plumbing that would possibly have been considered efficient on the *Mayflower*. There were some things you could put up with to gain the benefit and enjoyment of certain other things. The inconvenience was worth it most of the time.

"Yes," Susan agreed. "*I* understand. After all, this is only about the dozenth lost cause you've gotten yourself involved in since I've known you."

"Lost cause?" Holly's voice took on a testy edge. She heard an exasperated sigh on the other end of the line. "Lost cause?"

"You don't really think you can win against the infamous D. W. Branson, do you?"

Holly shifted in her chair, then switched the phone to her other ear. "I can try," she muttered. "At least I could have if he'd had the guts to show up."

"Look at it this way," Susan said with a hint of laughter. "Maybe it's a good thing he did cancel. How would it look if he arrived in the middle of one of your interviews and found out you had advertised in the paper for a weekend fiancé? Your credibility would be in shambles!"

"I guess you're right," Holly admitted. "I'll just have to deal with him when I get back from Valentine."

"I'm sure you will, but that's enough about D. W. Branson. Now tell me about the guy who's coming in for the interview. You know I've been nervous about this whole thing from the start."

"I keep telling you not to worry, I can take care of myself." Holly picked up the notes she had scribbled during the brief telephone conversation with the man the night before. "Actually, I don't know very much about him except that his name is David and he's a construction worker."

"Is that all?" Susan exclaimed. "I thought you were going to get as much information as you could!"

"Well . . ." she hedged. "I got a little distracted while he was on the phone."

Susan didn't bother to hide her exasperation. "The cats, right? I swear, Holly, if you didn't live in a jungle—"

"My house is not a jungle, Susan Martin! I happen to like plants and animals. They cause me far less trouble than my ex-husband ever did."

"No, it's just part zoo and part zoological garden. No wonder you need to advertise for a fiancé. What man in his right mind would go into a jungle infested with wild animals? Then there's that decrepit Volkswagen you drive as though the Indy 500 is a personal, everyday event."

Holly was laughing openly by then, ready to come back with an appropriate reply when she looked up and noticed the dark-haired man standing in the doorway, his shoulder propped against the frame. She had no idea how long he had been standing there, but from his relaxed pose it had obviously been some time. She sat up quickly. "Susan, I have to go," she said in a low voice. "He's here."

"Does he look promising?"

Quickly assessing the man, from his unruly black hair to his lean body clad in Levi's and a denim work shirt, she decided he was definitely promising. "Very," she whispered into the phone. "I'll see you tomorrow."

Branson watched as the young woman whispered something into the phone. She wasn't what he had expected—not at all like his tenth-grade English teacher—and she had one of the most appealing laughs he had heard in a long time. She hung up the phone and rose to come toward him, a hint of laughter still lingering on her lips. From the tone of her last letter, he wouldn't have been surprised if she had met him at the door with a loaded gun. He didn't trust her smile or the warmth in her honey-gold eyes. What was she up to?

Holly held out her hand in welcome, smiling warmly to put him at ease. His eyes were wary as he took her hand in his, but she couldn't blame him. She would be wary, too, of someone who had run an ad for a fiancé. His handshake was firm and strong and she felt a stir of excitement when she looked up into eyes the color of jade. *Yes*, she thought, *he'll do very well.*

Releasing his hand, she motioned to the chair beside her desk. "Have a seat, David, and we'll get started." She wondered why he had such a strange expression on his face. "You are David, aren't you?"

He nodded, wondering how she knew his first name. Nobody outside his immediate family had called him David for more years than he cared to remember. He felt his wariness being slowly replaced by a vague uneasiness and a great deal of curiosity.

"Ms. Nichols, I don't think—"

She panicked. Surely he couldn't be thinking of backing out. "Please, don't say no until you hear the details. I'm sure we can come to an understanding."

She seemed a little nervous, he thought, but what the hell. He was still trying to reconcile his image of H. C.

Nichols with the flesh-and-blood woman before him. He had watched her for several moments when he first arrived, taking advantage of her distraction to give her a thorough inspection. There was none of the smooth sophistication about her that he was accustomed to in the women of his acquaintance, but she was appealing in a way that both intrigued and mystified him. Her laughter had touched him on some basic level, as had the warmth in her eyes when she had greeted him.

Finally, he took the seat she offered, curious to hear what she had to say. He couldn't wait to find out what was going on behind those tawny eyes.

Holly shuffled her notes into a neat stack, attempting to arrange her thoughts, as well. Not wanting him to know how nervous she was, she kept her eyes averted as she began to speak. "First you must understand, this is strictly a business arrangement and not to be construed as a weekend of free sex."

David fought the urge to laugh as he crossed his arms over his chest and leaned back in his chair. This was getting more interesting by the minute. She obviously mistook him for someone else. He knew he should tell her, but an avid curiosity quickly overruled his good sense.

"Also, you are not to swear or make lewd suggestions in front of my family." She sounded so straitlaced and Victorian she was almost making herself nauseous. Lifting her head, she finally risked a glance at him. "Do you smoke or drink to excess?" Green eyes, fringed by the longest, blackest lashes she had ever seen, rested on her with an intensity that made her squirm.

He shook his head, his attention drawn to the light smattering of freckles across her nose. The flash of sensual awareness in her eyes belied the prim words she had been spouting, and Branson stifled a grin. He could listen to her go on and on all night, but his conscience was getting the better of him. H. C. Nichols might not bear a whit of resemblance to his tenth-grade English teacher, but she deserved to know the truth. He leaned forward slightly, intending to tell her before this went any further. "Ms. Nichols, I think you should know—"

She held up her hand to stop him. "Please, let me finish. If you have questions later, I'll be happy to answer them then. Do you understand everything so far?"

"I'm not sure," he sighed, giving in for the moment, "but do go on. I'm certain I'll get the drift." Surely a chance to get down to the reason for this meeting would soon present itself.

"As I told you on the telephone last night, I'll give you half the money, which comes to two hundred and fifty dollars, when we leave in the morning, the other half when we return." She cringed at the idea of crippling her savings account this way, but Michael had to be taught a lesson. Besides, she thought with a smug grin, it would be worth every penny if she could carry it off. She glanced at David and told herself to think of it as a contribution to charity. After all, he probably hadn't seen that much money in one lump sum in a very long time, if ever.

Meanwhile David was becoming uncomfortable. Was this even legal? "Ms. Nichols, I know I'm not sup-

posed to ask any questions, but I feel it imperative that
I be allowed to ask just one at this point."

Holly thought it odd that a construction worker
would use a word such as *imperative*, but there wasn't
time to explore that discrepancy right now. It was easy
to grant his simple request when those intriguing green
eyes of his were resting on her. She nodded her head.
"Of course."

"Where are we going?"

Hadn't that topic been covered last night? Trying to
keep the annoyance from her voice, she said, "Valentine, Nebraska."

David took a long, slow breath. Surely the lady was
joking. "What, pray tell, for?"

Holly closed her eyes, offering up a quick prayer for
patience, then decided she wasn't being quite fair.
Maybe he, too, had been distracted during their telephone conversation last night. After all, she hadn't even
caught his last name. Looking at him again, she could
see the confusion in his eyes and decided to give him the
benefit of the doubt.

Holly pushed her notes aside and sat back in the
chair. "I'm going to Valentine for my parents' silver
wedding anniversary. I advertised for a fiancé to go
with me." She could tell by the wary look on his face
that he still didn't understand. Maybe it would be better to tell the whole truth. "David, it's all a practical joke
on my brother." Her eyes suddenly flashed with wicked
humor. "Believe me, he deserves it! Are you game?"

He slumped back in the chair, rubbing his temples as
if to ward off an impending headache. How was he
going to get out of this? Actually, on second thought,

he was more than tempted to play along. This promised to be the most interesting experience he'd had in a long time. His practical side told him it was ridiculous to even consider it. His adventurous side, the part of him that had been mired in limbo for the past few months, urged him to go. At least he would have a chance to get to know her, prove to her that he wasn't the monster she thought him to be. If he told her the truth now, it would lower her opinion of him even further.

Still, his conscience screamed at him to be sensible. He stood to lose far more than he would gain by deceiving her. Deception had never been his way. It was far easier in the long run to be honest and upfront, but all it took to send his good intentions down the drain was for him to look into her pleading eyes, and he knew he was lost.

"By the way, David, what is your last name?"

"Didn't I tell you on the phone last night?" he asked warily.

She wished she could remove the doubt from his mind; he was vacillating and she wondered what she would do if he said no. "You might have, but one of my cats got tangled in the rhododendron and I missed a lot of the conversation trying to get him out."

David knew his curiosity had won out over his good sense when he heard himself saying, "It's Winslow, David Winslow."

"Well, David Winslow, I can't show up in Valentine with a fiancé who calls me Ms. Nichols. Maybe you should call me Holly."

"Holly it is," he said. Her name conjured up visions of mistletoe and candles, of gaily wrapped gifts and children's eyes full of wonder, of sleigh bells and laughter and peace on earth. He wondered where, behind the gentleness in her soft brown eyes, lurked the fire-breathing dragon who was after his head.

David Winslow did not seem to be the type of man who would answer a personal ad in the newspaper, Holly thought belatedly, but was too relieved by her good fortune to question his motives. Perhaps he was doing it for the money. His faded Levi's and denim work shirt had been around for a while, as had the dark blue windbreaker that didn't quite disguise the strength of his lean body. Glancing at his unruly black hair, she thought maybe he would use some of the money for a haircut. He seemed nice, in a quiet, reserved way. She couldn't help but wonder if he ever laughed.

"Well, David," she said at last, "I think this is going to work out well. If you don't have any plans for this evening, I'd like to take you out to dinner and tell you a little about my family and what will be going on this weekend. The more background you have, the more chance we'll have of pulling this off."

David glanced down at his dusty clothes, he had been come directly from the civic center construction site where he'd spent most of the afternoon. "I'm afraid I'm not dressed for dinner," he said. Besides, what if they ran into someone he knew? He didn't know what her preferences were when it came to dining out, but he couldn't chance having his identity revealed before he was ready.

Reaching into the bottom drawer of her desk to get her purse, she remarked, "No problem. Where we're going, the dress code doesn't extend beyond 'no shoes, no shirt, no service.'"

Holly stood and walked toward the door. "I'd like to stop by my house first and change clothes. It won't take long." Maybe he would be more at ease if she were dressed more casually. She knew *she* would be more comfortable. The tailored navy blue suit and silk blouse she wore looked incongruous next to his Levi's and work shirt.

David followed her, unable to stop himself from admiring the way her small, softly rounded body filled out the stylish suit. For a man who had always been attracted to tall, willowy model types, he was disturbed by the definite stirring of male interest unfolding inside him. *Dangerous, Branson*, he warned himself, *you're treading on thin ice.*

He warily watched her as they left the building and stepped outside into the soft May evening, coming to a halt beside the most decrepit-looking Volkswagen it had ever been his misfortune to see. It had once been red but had faded to a dull, lusterless orange. The left front fender was light blue, the driver's door was black and the back bumper was missing completely.

Holly unlocked the door, watching out of the corner of her eye as he circled around the back, openly perusing her car with trepidation. Finally, he looked at her over the top of the small vehicle.

"Does this thing really run?"

Accustomed to derogatory remarks about her car, she shrugged. "It gets me where I want to go." She knew she needed a new car; this one couldn't last much longer. But there were so many other things on which she'd rather spend her money.

Unlocking the door, she got in and reached over to unlock the opposite door for David. After buckling her seat belt, she started the engine.

David smothered a gasp as Holly shifted gears and roared out of the parking lot with a squeal of tires.

"I don't live far from here so we'll be there in just a few moments." Holly braked to a halt at a stop sign and unbuttoned her suit jacket, looking forward to slipping into something more comfortable.

She roared away from the stop sign, shifting quickly into second and then third gear. "How long have you lived in Indianapolis?" she asked, barely slowing down to negotiate a turn.

"Since I was fifteen," he ground out through clenched teeth. "I've survived nearly twenty years in this town, Ms. Nichols. If at all possible, I would like to make it through a few more."

"Were you born here?"

"No, I was born in Terre Haute," he said, sucking in his breath as a slow-moving vehicle pulled into their path. It wasn't that David was frightened by Holly's driving. Actually, he was stunned. She was very good behind the wheel, if a little fast. She just didn't bear any resemblance to a race-car driver.

Holly shifted into second, whipped around the car ahead and moved smoothly back into her own lane. A few minutes later she pulled into a blacktopped driveway beside a modest two-storey house and turned off the ignition.

David breathed a sigh of relief and turned to face her, wondering if she really did know who he was and had chosen her own brand of revenge. "Just when did you sign a suicide pact with this car?"

Her eyes widened in innocent surprise. "Did my driving upset you?"

"Upset?" he asked in a deceptively bland voice. "Why would I be upset? One of my fondest wishes is to be splattered all over the streets of Indianapolis."

Susan was always telling her she was a menace when she got behind the wheel of a car, but Holly brushed it off, having too much confidence in her skill to listen. She did admit to a tendency to drive a little fast sometimes.

"I'm sorry, David," she murmured. "Truly I am. I wasn't thinking."

"Lady, with you behind the wheel, this car should be declared a lethal weapon."

"I said I was sorry!" she snapped, her golden eyes flashing with indignation. Had she looked at him directly, she would have seen the humor lurking in his eyes. "Besides, I got us here, didn't I?"

David shifted his gaze from her to look out the window. This quiet neighborhood was yet another surprise. The lawns and trees along the wide avenue sported a fresh shade of spring green in the gathering twilight. Tulips and daffodils added bright spots of color along brick or cement sidewalks.

He turned to Holly. "This is where you live?"

She eyed him cautiously, accustomed to negative reactions to her choice of neighborhood. She was pleased to see approval in his eyes.

"I knew what I wanted when I decided to invest in a house," she said. "You wouldn't believe the hours I wasted while real estate people dragged me from one condominium to another, trying to convince me that's where I belonged. I found this house when I was out driving around one day."

"I'm surprised you slowed down long enough to notice it."

Holly started to make a sharp retort, then noticed the teasing light in his eyes and felt her heart take a funny little leap. Since her divorce three years ago, she had become adept at keeping men at arm's length. Now she found herself wanting to know much more about this man who had landed in her life in such an unorthodox fashion.

To cover her confusion, she didn't answer but got out of the car and walked up to her front door, making a show of digging around in her purse for her keys. It would never do for David to see just how undone she was. He wouldn't understand her reaction. How could he? Even she didn't understand it.

Annoyed with herself, Holly finally came up with the key and unlocked the front door. She could feel David's presence behind her, was aware of him as she hadn't been aware of any man in a very long time. As she stepped into the cool foyer, she prayed he would have no inkling of the effect he had on her. It was important that she maintain at least a semblance of control over this situation, at least for the weekend.

Holly smiled as a huge, furry monster bounded down the hallway and skidded to a stop at her feet.

"Good Lord! What is that?"

Holly patted the German shepherd and said, "This is Brewster." Glancing over her shoulder, she stifled a grin at the look on David's face. It wasn't exactly fear—she had a feeling there wasn't much that would frighten David Winslow—but more like healthy respect. "Don't worry," she assured him, "Brewster won't bite unless I tell him to."

"What do you mean by that?"

"He's trained for protection, so he'll only attack if I order him to. Otherwise, he's a big marshmallow."

"Marshmallows don't have teeth," David stated matter-of-factly.

Holly just chuckled, commanded Brewster to lie down and walked through an archway that led to the living room. Kicking off her high-heeled pumps, she motioned toward the couch. "Make yourself comfortable while I go change."

David followed Holly into the living room, his attention tuned to the big dog watching him with alert, intelligent brown eyes. "Are you going to leave me alone with him?" he asked, wanting to make friends with the dog but not wishing to lose a hand in the process.

Holly heard the cautious note in David's voice and smiled inwardly. "I told you, he won't attack unless I tell him to, or if you try to make off with the family silver while I'm upstairs." With that, she flashed a smile and disappeared down the hallway.

David heard her footsteps on the stairs, his eyes still on the archway through which she had disappeared, then he turned to survey the warm, inviting living room, finding it a reflection of the woman who lived there. Though he had just met Holly, he could see her personality everywhere as he circled the room, stopping to admire the delicate figurines on the gleaming mantel above the corner fireplace; running his hand over the nubby texture of cream-colored cushions on the couch; smiling at the profusion of plants hanging from the high ceiling or placed on end tables and plant stands around the room.

He thrust his hands into the pockets of his windbreaker and wandered over to the stereo system in the corner. He flipped through Holly's extensive record collection, his eyes growing pensive as he read the titles and the names of the artists. It seemed he and Holly shared an amazingly similar taste in music; everything from Alabama to Mantovani.

"Are you ready to go?"

He turned at the sound of her voice, his heart slamming into his chest when she greeted him with a warm smile. Pale blue jeans and a gold sweater showed off her rounded curves to perfection. She wore little makeup, just a touch of mascara and some shiny lip gloss that made him wonder if her lips tasted as sweet as they looked. The lady was wreaking havoc on his senses.

Holly saw the flash of desire in his eyes and her throat went dry. It was difficult to think of this as a business arrangement when her thoughts were anything but businesslike. She was wondering what it would be like to kiss him.

Stupid! she thought, tearing her gaze from him and spinning around to walk on legs that were suddenly weak and rubbery. *You're an idiot, Holly Carol Nichols, to even think such insane thoughts. You adver-*

*tised for this man, for heaven's sake! How can you even
think the things you're thinking!*

She was almost to the car before she realized she had
left David standing alone in the middle of the living
room. Coming to a halt, she turned around, startled to
find him right behind her. She stared at him for a long
moment, fighting to keep her wayward thoughts under control, then said the first thing that came to her
mind.

"Did you lock the door?"

"Who would break in with that beast in there?" he
asked.

"Brewster isn't a beast."

"Right," David agreed easily. "He's a marshmallow
with teeth."

Holly grinned, feeling the tension ease between them.
"Where did you get a name like Brewster?"

She went around the car to the driver's side, giving
him an impish look. "I named him after Brewster Baker in the movie *Six Pack*."

"What is a Brewster Baker?"

"He was a race-car driver."

David rolled his eyes. "I should have known!"

Holly glared at him over the top of her car. "Are you
going to make some more smart remarks about my
driving? I promise I'll take it easier on your fragile
nerves."

He reached for the door handle. "Good! I'd hate to
have to bail out in self-defence and leave you with the
guilt of my untimely death on your conscience."

2

"McDONALD'S? We're having dinner at McDonald's?" David stared at the famous golden arches in disbelief.

"Why, David Winslow! Don't tell me you've never suffered from a Big Mac attack!"

He felt another twinge of conscience at her use of that name. He wondered if he could really carry this off. "I can honestly say I can't remember the last time I suffered from a Big Mac attack, but the way this evening has gone so far, this shouldn't come as any surprise." Humor flickered momentarily across his face and a hint of a smile quirked his lips.

"Well, you happened to catch me on my junk-food night."

"I caught you? I think you have your pronouns mixed up."

Holly looked up at him, her chin set at a stubborn angle. "Do you want dinner or not?"

David lifted his gaze once again to the golden arches soaring into the night sky and shrugged. "You're the boss," he said, smiling inwardly when he glanced down in time to see the self-satisfied smile on her face.

Once inside the brightly lit fast-food restaurant, David went in search of a vacant table while Holly went to get their food. At least here he wouldn't have to worry about running into anyone he knew.

Taking a seat by the window, he gazed out at the masses of people bustling about the busy shopping mall. This mall had been his first major project, ten years ago, marking the beginning of D. W. Branson Development's financial success. There had been other malls, some larger and more elaborate, but none would ever be as special as this one. David hadn't been here since the opening ceremony was held on a cold, cloudy February day. He had meant to come back. There just never seemed to be enough time.

Life had become easier after this mall was completed. Not only had it marked a beginning for his business, but it had meant college for his brothers and sisters, the means by which to purchase a house and to achieve a certain amount of financial freedom.

But what did all of it mean? David reached up to massage the back of his neck. Tension seemed to be a part of his life he couldn't avoid. His brothers and sisters were grown now, and he was making more money than he could spend in one lifetime, so why wasn't he enjoying the freedom? Why was he suffering from this special version of empty-nest syndrome? Then there was Nick. His youngest brother had called several months ago to tell David he was quitting college. David had tried his best to talk Nick into staying in school but hadn't succeeded. Now Nick's infrequent telephone calls as he traveled about the country on his motorcycle were his only contact.

"I hope strawberry is all right with you."

He jumped, jerking his head around to stare at Holly as if she were an apparition. "Pardon me?"

She set the food-lane tray on the table and took the seat across from him. Picking up one of the paper cups from the tray, she handed it to him. "Strawberry," she said gently, wondering anew at the depth of loneliness in his eyes. "Is that okay?"

David nodded, staring at the cup for a moment before shifting his attention to the inordinate amount of food on the tray. "Did you invite the neighborhood?"

"I guess I should have warned you," she said with a slight smile. "When I pig out, I go all the way." She handed him a Big Mac and a large order of fries, then took the same for herself.

"What were you thinking about just now?" she asked, remembering the faraway look in his eyes as he stared out at the mall.

"I was watching the people."

She took a sip of her shake, eyeing him closely. "You looked as if you'd never seen a shopping mall before."

"I haven't had much time for shopping malls—or McDonald's, either," he confessed. "Except for building them." His lips spread in a grin, the closest to a real smile he had given her all evening. "Shopping malls, not McDonald's."

Holly's Big Mac stopped halfway to her mouth. "You build shopping malls?"

He only shrugged nonchalantly. "I've worked on a few." He watched her as she ate, noting how the bright lights brought out the golden highlights in her hair. There was something soft and gentle about her, yet she was bright, intelligent, every bit the successful businesswoman if the looks of her office were any indication. He wrestled with the urge to lean over and kiss away the dollop of catsup at the corner of her mouth. "Tell me about your family," he said instead. "Which one are you? Youngest? Oldest? Middle?"

Holly thought for a minute. "I used to be number three, but I dropped to number five when Mom and Dad got married."

David stared at her, his eyes mirroring his confusion. "Would you like to run that by me again?"

"My real father, or my biological father if you prefer, left before I was born. My mom married Sam when I was one. He was a widower with two kids of his own. I have a full brother and sister, a half brother and sister and a stepbrother and sister. With Mom and Sam it was a case of your kids, my kids and our kids, but we don't pay much attention to technicalities. We're just family. Sam is the only real father I've ever known."

"He must be quite a man."

"He is," Holly said. "He and my mother have known each other all their lives. Everyone knows everyone else in Valentine. Especially Sam. He owns a grocery store there."

"He would have to just to be able to feed you," David muttered, watching with interest as Holly popped the last bite of hamburger into her mouth and washed it down with a drink of her shake.

"My older brother, Joe, designs, builds and drives racing cars. In fact, he's in town this month for the 500. He's married to a mechanic he met in Atlanta. He and Sandy are expecting their first baby in July." Holly reached for a cherry pie and offered it to David, but he declined. "Then there's Brianny. She's an interstate truck driver and is married to a dentist she met when she developed an impacted wisdom tooth in Denver. They have a little girl, Amy, who is two years old." Her eyes sparkled with humor.

"Where does a little thing like you put all that food?"

Holly sat back in her chair with a sigh of content-ment. "I told you I have a tendency to overdo when it comes to junk food." Her brow wrinkled in concentra-tion. "Let's see. Where was I?"

"Don't ask me!"

"Ah, Louisa! She and her husband, Rob, live in Om-aha. They have a motorcycle shop and two kids, both boys. Rob designed a racing wheel for motorcycles a couple of years ago and they travel all over the coun-try selling them. Their boys have started racing, too. Bobby is eight and Kevin is nine."

Holly shifted her position slightly, her eyes resting on David. She couldn't help but wonder what was going on behind those incredible eyes of his. Not only did he seem unintimidated by what she was telling him, but he acted as though he were actually interested in every word she said.

"That leaves the twins, Tina and Tim," she said after a while. "They're both in school at the University of Nebraska. Tina wants to become a midwife and work on the Sioux reservation in South Dakota. Tim is studying agricultural science, plays football and trav-els the rodeo circuit during the summer." Holly grinned cheekily. "I think that covers it. Do you think you can remember all that?"

He shook his head, his lips twitching in amusement. "I think you lost me somewhere between Denver and Omaha."

"I almost forgot Michael!" she groaned, pressing her hand to her forehead in dismay.

"I'm not sure I should ask, but who is Michael?"

"He's in fourth place, just ahead of me. He's a minister."

"A minister?" David couldn't suppress a grin. "I'm glad to hear there's one normal one in the group."

Holly let out a very unladylike snort. "That's what Michael would like everyone to believe, but I grew up with him! I could spend the rest of tonight telling you stories about the 'normal' one. We've been playing jokes on each other since we were kids." Her lips spread in a wide grin and her eyes gleamed with mischief. "This may be the best one yet. The whole plot of my bringing a fiancé home for the weekend is for his benefit. The whole family is in on it."

David gazed at her intently, intrigued by the devious expression on her face. "What did Michael do to incur your wrath?" He would be willing to bet Michael wasn't threatening to tear a building down around her head.

Holly's eyes narrowed. "I went home at Easter, only to discover that Michael had been spreading a story about me being engaged to some guy here in Indianapolis. He'd been here for a convention a few weeks before and we went out to dinner together. Unfortunately, we happened to run into one of my clients. He was a real jerk, always trying to get me to go out with him. I wasn't the least bit interested. He had an ego the size of Indiana, with nothing to back it up. Anyway, when Michael and I saw him, he started in on me again, even getting Michael into the act. Of course, he had no idea

Michael was loving every minute of watching his little sister squirm."

"After I finally got rid of the guy, Michael teased me unmercifully until I threatened to deck him right in the middle of the restaurant." Holly paused to gaze suspiciously at David. "If you laugh, I'll deck *you* right in the middle of *this* restaurant!" After a minute, content that David had contained the merriment she had seen dancing in his eyes, she went on. "Imagine my surprise when I arrived home for Easter to find the entire family buzzing with the news of my impending engagement! I could have throttled Michael. He had everyone convinced that I was on my way down the aisle." Holly sat back with a look of smug satisfaction on her face. "That's why my family is so willing to help me get back at him. They were all taken in by his story. My sister Brianny, though, is the only one who knows how I'm acquiring this fiancé. She plotted the whole thing. I can't wait to see the look on Michael's face when I arrive with a fiancé in tow."

She sat up straight, her gaze roaming David's face curiously. "Doesn't my family intimidate you at all?"

Eyeing the stack of styrofoam and cardboard cartons, paper cups and other discarded rubbish on the tray, he shook his head and grinned. "I'm more intimidated by the amount of food you put away than by your family. You should be in the *Guinness Book of World Records*."

She laughed, entranced with the realization that he was actually teasing her. Maybe he did have a sense of humor after all.

"All I can say," David stated, shaking his head in disbelief, "is that between your family and mine, it's a good thing we're not really getting married or we'd have to rent the Indy racetrack for the ceremony."

Holly's eyes widened in surprise. "You have a family?" He seemed like such a loner, it hadn't occurred to her to ask him about a family.

David leaned forward, resting his forearms on the table, his eyes glinting with humor. "How did you think I got here, Holly, by Western Union?" he asked softly.

Her fingers itched to touch him. She could fall so easily under his spell if she allowed herself to. But she didn't dare. If he had a family, what had put that loneliness in his eyes? Still, she knew that there were some kinds of loneliness that even a loving family couldn't erase. Maybe, too, he wasn't as close to his family as she was to hers. Some families were like that.

"I guess I didn't think about it at all," she said at last. "You seem like such a . . . a . . . I'm sorry," she stammered.

He reached out and wrapped his hand around one of hers. "A loner?"

She nodded, allowing her slender fingers to curl around David's strong ones. It felt so good, and so very, very right.

Holly was right, he thought with a pang of regret. His sister Cheryl often accused him of the same thing. He had been a loner for most of his life, ever since his parents were killed in a car accident when he was sixteen. His world went to hell with that accident. He'd woken up in a hospital to find his parents gone and his brothers and sisters dispersed to various foster homes around the state.

It had taken a long time and a lot of determination for him to reach the point where he could gather them all up into a family again. But that nagging sense of loneliness never fully left him. Even when they all came home, once again filling his rambling house with noise and laughter, the loneliness still haunted him. The past couple of years had been the worst, ever since Nick left for college. Now, when he looked at Holly, when he felt the gentleness of her gaze and the warmth of her laughter, he didn't feel quite so empty, or lonely, and that scared the hell out of him. He couldn't get involved with her, not this particular woman. His intentions in playing along with her off-the-wall scheme had been solely to allow her to get to know him as a human being and, therefore, to be able to convince her he wasn't the devil incarnate. To think there could ever be a relationship between them, other than business, was crazy.

He abruptly released her hand and looked away. "Well, you're right," he said gruffly when he brought his gaze back to her. "Despite having four brothers and two sisters, I am pretty much a loner. I find it much safer that way."

Holly didn't believe it for a moment. She knew about barriers. Hadn't she erected a good number of her own since her divorce? It was easy to identify the distance he put between them as just another barrier. If circumstances were different, she would see how much of that barrier she could tear down. The attraction between them was too strong to deny, yet both were working very hard at doing just that.

"Where are your parents?"

"They're dead." David stood abruptly and picked up the tray that was piled high with the remains of their meal. "If you've finished stuffing yourself," he said with a faint smile, "maybe we'd better go."

She didn't want to go. She wanted to stay right here in McDonald's and hear his entire life story. She wanted to know everything there was to know about David Winslow. Instead, she rose to her feet, trying not to think about how much she missed the warmth of his hand wrapped around hers. He was far too appealing, far too intriguing for her peace of mind. She was treading on very dangerous ground.

They were almost to the exit when Holly stopped suddenly. "Wait a minute! I want to get a box of cookies before we leave." Actually she needed to put a little distance between herself and David, if just for a few minutes. The cookies were a weak excuse, but other than the feminine ploy of freshening her makeup and escaping into the ladies' room, it was the best she could come up with.

"I don't believe this," he groaned, giving her a crooked grin that set her heart to beating in double time. "I'll wait for you outside."

A few minutes later, with a box of cookies in her purse and another self-lecture under her belt, Holly pushed the glass door open and looked around for David. He stood several feet away, his hands tucked into the back pockets of his jeans, once again watching the people moving about the vast mall.

"Want me to take you on a tour?" she asked, coming up to stand beside him.

She isn't my type at all, David told himself, shoving his hands deeper into his pockets to keep from reaching out and touching each and every freckle that dotted her pert nose. He had always been attracted to women who were very sophisticated, hadn't he? He definitely did not go for petite, kooky women who could put away enough junk food in one sitting to feed the entire Indianapolis Colts football team.

"Did you get your box of cookies?" he asked with a small smile, feeling an overwhelming urge to kiss her right there in front of McDonald's.

"Sure did," she answered, patting the bulging purse slung over her shoulder. Then, tucking her arm through his, she nodded toward the mall. "Come on. Let's go window-shopping." Holly ignored the tiny voice inside her that reminded her of the lecture she had just delivered to herself, a lecture that had thoroughly covered each and every reason why she could not become involved with David Winslow. Instead, she found herself enjoying the feel of his muscular arm beneath her fingertips.

"How can you even walk after all that food you put away?" he teased her. "I keep waiting for you to self-destruct before my very eyes."

"I hope you don't think I eat like that all the time! Believe me, I'll pay for it tomorrow. It'll be back to yogurt and bean sprouts."

"You'll be at your parents' house tomorrow," he reminded her as they entered the mall. "Don't tell me your mother is serving yogurt and bean sprouts! I'll have to take along some emergency rations."

Holly rolled her eyes in dismay. "How could I have forgotten! My mother wouldn't be caught dead putting yogurt and bean sprouts on the table. I'll really have to crash diet next week."

David finally succumbed to temptation, moving his arm so that her hand slid down to rest in his. "Tell me, Holly, how did you end up in Indianapolis from Valentine, Nebraska?"

"Very scientifically," she said with a grin. "I closed my eyes and picked it out on a map."

As they walked along, pausing momentarily to look in this or that window, she answered David's questions about her career as a chartered life underwriter and tried not to be concerned about his evasiveness when she asked him similar questions about his own career.

They came to a jewelry store and David tugged her to a stop. There was a strange light in his eyes when he said, "Come on, Holly, pick out your engagement ring."

Willing to go along with his mood, Holly stepped up to the window and peered through the glass at the magnificent display of diamonds, emeralds and rubies. David's arm came to rest across her shoulders, sending a shock wave of heat through her veins. She was more entranced by their reflection in the window glass than by the dazzling array of gems on the other side. She could feel his warm breath on her temple as he surveyed the sparkling jewels spread out before them.

"If you had your choice, which one would you pick?"

"I don't know," she managed to say, unable to concentrate on anything as mundane as precious gems when the strong line of his jaw was so close and so very tempting.

"Come on, spoilsport," he insisted, giving her a quick hug. "Every red-blooded American woman loves to flash a big rock in her friends' faces just to prove what a great catch she's made."

An old bitterness welled up inside her as she shrugged out of David's embrace. She fought the feeling, but he could still see a trace of it in her eyes as she tilted her head to look up at him. "Not every woman, David," she said in a carefully controlled voice. "My ex-husband bought me a diamond the size of a radish, but it didn't keep him from an endless stream of women during the two years we were married."

Appalled, Holly felt her face flush with embarrassment when she realized what she had said. What had possessed her to reveal such a thing, and to a near stranger at that? The flush deepened as David's own eyes shadowed with self-disgust. She hadn't meant to cause him discomfort, but she didn't like the insinuation he had made, either. She had to wonder what kind of women he had known in his life.

"I'm sorry," she said after a long, strained minute, groping for a smile to relieve the tension in the air.

"I'm the one who should apologize," he said, his voice like fine sandpaper. He wondered what kind of monster she'd been married to. He could kick himself for his stupidity. It was as if he were trying to prove that she was, after all, like the other women he knew, women who, unfortunately, measured a person by what he owned instead of by who and what he was. It was in his own self-defense that he had tried to prove Holly wasn't so different after all. There were scars hidden beneath Holly Nichols's sunny disposition, and a trace of sadness lurked in her laughing eyes. Again he felt a tug of awareness that both intrigued and troubled him. He felt a strong urge to take her in his arms and kiss away that sadness, but sensed she would not welcome such a gesture from him, especially now.

David's simple apology went straight to her heart. Rick had never apologized to her for anything, not even when she had arrived home one afternoon to find him in bed, their bed, with his latest secretary.

Holly took a deep breath, allowing herself to relax and regain her sense of perspective, and her sense of humor. She couldn't understand or explain her overreaction to David's remark. And why should she care what kind of women he had known in his life? It was none of her business and she had no intention of becoming involved.

From behind her, Holly heard the rousing noise of a video arcade. "Come on, Winslow," she urged lightly. "Let's get an Orange Julius and then I'll beat you at Pac-Man." Brushing past him, she kept her eyes straight ahead, ignoring the way her pulse leaped as David fell into step beside her.

"An Orange Julius sounds suspiciously like food," he said in a voice rippling with laughter. "Holly, how can you possibly want anything to eat?"

She stopped in her tracks, staring up at him in disbelief. "David Winslow, you don't eat an Orange Julius, you drink it. Now don't tell me you've never had one."

"Okay, I won't tell you I've never had one."

She shook her head and walked off, returning in a few minutes with two frothy drinks in her hands. Tilting her head toward some benches nearby, she said, "Let's sit down for a few minutes. All that shopping has worn me out."

She didn't look worn-out to David. She looked fresh and alive and very, very appealing. When they sat down he took a tentative taste of the drink she handed him and nodded his head in approval. "This is pretty good. I'll have to try it sometime when I'm really hungry."

Her eyes widened in shock. "Omigod, you were serious! You really haven't had one, have you?"

"I told you, Holly, I don't spend much time in shopping malls except to build them."

"Where do you get your clothes?" Maybe at Goodwill, she thought wickedly, eyeing his faded Levi's and well-worn work shirt.

"I have someone who does my shopping for me," he said evasively, pretending an absorbing interest in the ebb and flow of people around them. He couldn't very well tell her that his tailor came to him, that all he had to do was pick up a telephone and the finest clothiers in the city were at his beck and call.

Holly felt a cold chill work its way up her spine. Was it a wife who bought his clothes for him? The thought had not occurred to her. A married man wouldn't have answered her ad. Would he?

"Are you married?" she asked, staring at the swirl of foam in her cup as she stirred it with the straw. She didn't want to consider why his answer was so important to her.

An expression of genuine surprise crossed his face. "Good heavens, no!" David was shocked at how sharp he sounded, but she had really thrown him a curve with that question.

Holly exhaled what she hoped was an unnoticeable sigh of relief. She looked up at David and was immediately captured by the desire flaring in his incredible eyes. They were seated on a bench in the middle of a thriving mall, with dozens of people milling around, yet Holly felt as though they were the only two people in the world. All her senses were attuned to the attractive, mysterious man seated next to her. He reached up to trace the curve of her cheek with a strong, callused finger and she shuddered.

"Would it matter so very much if I were?" he whispered in a rough voice. "After all, this is strictly a business arrangement."

Who had been dumb enough to put such a ridiculous restriction on this glorious act of fate? Her breath caught in her throat as his finger slid along the line of her jaw, coming to rest on the point of her chin. Mesmerized by the emerald eyes holding her captive, Holly found it difficult to speak.

"How would it look," she said, almost in a whisper, "if I took off for a weekend with a married man?"

"A lot of women would think nothing of it."

"I'm not your average, run-of-the-mill woman," she murmured. "Some people think I'm weird."

David chuckled, scanning her elfin face feature by feature, from her wide, tawny eyes, to her pert nose, and finally to her full, moist lips. "Not weird," he denied softly. "Unique, maybe, but not weird." She was more than unique, he thought, she was refreshing. He could feel something unwinding inside of himself that had been coiled tight for far too long.

David's eyes were doing a slow burn, and Holly knew she had to do something to break the spell. If she didn't, he would kiss her right here in the mall with a good portion of Indianapolis looking on. She was torn between craving the feel of his mouth on hers and fear at what would happen to her afterward.

"Betcha I can beat you at Pac-Man," she said with forced lightness.

He stared at her in confusion, then burst into laughter. Holly felt the warmth and force of it clear down to her toes. His laugh, though a long time coming, had been worth waiting for. She sat still, watching him and letting the joy and wonder of it wash over her. He looked younger, more relaxed and so very attractive.

"Holly," he finally managed to say, "I know you're going to find this difficult to believe, but I've never played Pac-Man in my life! I have every confidence that not only will you beat me, you'll humiliate me!"

Holly stood up and tossed her empty cup into a nearby trash can, then grabbed David's hand and towed him toward the noisy arcade. "Your education is sorely lacking, my man," she teased, glad to have broken the sexual tension that had sprung up between them. She knew they would have to deal with it in time—the attraction was too strong to be denied for very long—but for now, with the sound of his laughter still ringing in her heart, she wanted to teach him how to have fun.

When they entered the brightly lit arcade, a barrage of bleeps, bongs, whines, whings and rock music assaulted them. David tugged on her hand, bending down to yell in her ear. "Do people come out of these places alive?"

"Of course, silly," she mouthed, directing his attention to a nearby video machine. "I have to get some tokens, then I'll teach you how to play some of the games."

"Meeting you has been a real learning experience already," he chuckled. "I can't wait to see what the next lesson brings."

"I intend to take full advantage of your inexperience. Wait here, I'll be right back."

When she returned with a handful of tokens, David was standing in front of the machine, rubbing his chin thoughtfully. Holly hoped she wasn't on the verge of making a complete fool of herself. It had been a long time since she had indulged in video games.

David was a fast learner, Holly decided an hour later when the score stood at two games each.

"Beginner's luck," she sniffed. "Now we'll play Pac-Man for the championship! I feel it only fair to warn you, it's my best game."

"What does the winner get?" David asked, having the time of his life.

Holly thought for a moment, not daring to say that she wouldn't mind getting the kiss she hadn't gotten in the mall. "The winner can drive home."

"That gives me real incentive," he stated dryly, but he didn't really care. His naturally competitive spirit was in full swing.

A half hour later Holly stared at the video screen in stunned dismay. He had beat her by fifty points! Fifty lousy points! His whoop of delight could be heard all over the arcade.

"How did you do that?" she demanded, miffed at getting beaten by a rank amateur.

He grinned engagingly, bending his head to drop a brief kiss on her parted lips. "State secret! Now, hand over the keys, my little speed demon."

Holly was so shaken she didn't even argue. He had won fair and square. At least she would have to give him the benefit of the doubt. It wasn't losing that had her so unnerved, it was his kiss. Soft and fleeting though it had been, it had left an indelible impression on her lips and on her heart. It had lasted only as long as a heartbeat, yet the taste and feel of it lingered on her lips long after they'd left the shopping mall behind them.

3

THEY WERE two blocks from her house before Holly realized they should be going back downtown to her office building.

"What about your car?" She risked a glance at David. He had been as quiet as she since they left the mall.

"I'll call a cab from your place," he answered quickly, glancing over at her before turning his attention back to the road. "If that's all right with you."

"I could drive you. There's no sense wasting money on a cab."

He gave a low chuckle. "I'm not about to turn you loose on the innocent citizens of this city at this time of night."

Biting back a sharp retort, Holly turned to gaze out the window at the darkness. She didn't want the evening to end, yet she was frightened of the feelings she was already having for David. She had just met him, yet she felt comfortable with him in a way that was unsettling, and she knew so very little about him, aside from the fact that he came from a large family, did construction work, used words like *imperative*, had been born in Terre Haute, had the most marvelous eyes she had ever encountered, and his touch set her on fire....

"What are you thinking about?" he asked in a deceptively casual voice. The quiet tension in the air since leaving the mall had not gone unnoticed by David. The forced intimacy of the small car did nothing to ease matters, either. Every time he shifted gears he could feel the warmth of her thigh, even though she was very careful to move enough so that he didn't touch her. Though he couldn't see her face, David sensed the tautness in her small body, felt the same confusion he knew she must be feeling. Never had a kiss had such an effect on him. And it hadn't even been a real kiss, more of a suggestion of one. It hadn't been nearly enough. The taste of her lingered, leaving him hungering for more. Now, as he pulled into her driveway, he was reluctant for the evening to end.

"Nothing important," she murmured in answer to his question. She couldn't very well say she was wondering what a real kiss from him would be like. Holly was startled to discover they had arrived at her house. "Come on in and have some coffee while you wait for your cab. Sometimes they can take a while."

Brewster greeted them at the door and Holly left David to make his call while she went into the kitchen to put on a pot of coffee. The call must not have taken long because she could hear him moving around in the other room as she scooped coffee into the basket and filled the reservoir with water. When the soft sounds of Barry Manilow drifted into the kitchen, she smiled. It was one of her favorite albums.

While the coffee perked, Holly filled a watering can and watered the profusion of plants in the greenhouse window over the sink. Hearing a noise behind her, she turned around. He was leaning against the door frame, looking exactly as he had at her office a few hours ago, yet so very different. Now he was familiar, almost like an old friend. Holly pondered that for a moment, then knew it was true. David was like an old and trusted friend, while still retaining an aura of mystery that intrigued and beckoned her. He had removed his jacket and the rolled-up sleeves of his shirt revealed a sinewy length of sun-bronzed arm.

"Did you make your call?" she asked, setting the watering can on the tile counter.

"The line was busy." He strolled into the room, taking a quick survey of the warm, cozy kitchen with its knotty pine cabinets and gleaming almond appliances. "It was very dangerous to do what you did, Holly Nichols," he stated softly.

Confused, she leaned against the counter and mentally catalogued everything they'd done. "What was dangerous about going to McDonald's and an arcade?"

"I'm talking about that ad you ran," he stated. "There's no telling what kind of weirdo characters you could have attracted."

Remembering the candidates she had interviewed earlier that day, Holly stifled a laugh. They had been weird all right, but none had seemed dangerous to her. There were many kinds of danger, she thought, watching David roam about her kitchen. Funny, it had never seemed so small before.

"I guess I was lucky," she murmured as her eyes met his.

He moved slowly toward her, an unreadable light in his eyes. "You don't know anything about me, Holly," he said in a low voice. "For all you know I could be some kind of pervert. I could have answered that ad just for an excuse to get into your house to rape, ravish or mutilate your lovely body."

Her heart leaped into her throat as he came to a halt a few inches from her. Placing a hand on either side of her, he trapped her against the counter.

"Did . . . did you?" she whispered huskily, captured again by the smoky look in his jade green eyes. She felt no fear, only a swift, hot longing to be in his arms.

"No," he admitted softly, then shrugged slightly, his eyes gleaming with a devilish delight. "Well, maybe one out of the three." His lips hovered near hers. "Holly Nichols, you are like a breath of fresh air. I can't remember when I've spent a more interesting evening."

Holly recognized the look in his eyes and tried to resist, knowing it was futile. "This is supposed to be business!" She gasped as his lips trailed across her cheek to her hairline.

"I've never believed in mixing business with pleasure, but—" his lips brushed her temple with tantalizing softness "—maybe I'll have to change my habits."

"I even have a contract...David!" He moved to catch her bottom lip between his teeth.

"What kind of contract?" He found it difficult to concentrate on anything but the taste and scent of her soft skin.

Holly grasped the edge of the counter behind her with both hands to keep from touching the lean body that was pressing against her so provocatively. She knew if she touched him she would be lost. She tried to concentrate on the contract. "To cover all the points I mentioned at the office." His warm mouth nuzzled the sensitive area below her ear before he lifted his head to gaze down at her.

"You mean the trip to Nebraska?"

She nodded, entranced by the tiny lines feathering out from the corners of his eyes and the trace of silver at his temples.

"What time period does the contract cover?" He wasn't really concerned about the contract. He had gained a lot of experience with contracts over the years and found he could make most of them work to his advantage. Of course, he wasn't about to tell her that.

"From the time we leave for Omaha tomorrow until we return on Sunday evening." Why were they discussing such a mundane subject when what he had been doing with his mouth was so much more interesting?

His arms slipped around her waist and he drew her against his hard muscled frame. "Good!" he exclaimed softly. "That gives us about twelve hours."

Holly's eyes drifted shut as his mouth finally settled on hers in a gentle, exploring kiss. Waves of emotion swept over her as she succumbed to his tender assault. It had been well over three years since she had felt desire for any man, but David was kindling a fire Holly hadn't even known existed. Her arms found their way around his neck and she moved against him, reveling in his lean strength and the magic he was working on her all-too-willing mouth.

From the moment his lips met hers, David knew he could lose himself in this woman. She filled his arms with warmth and softness, and when her lips parted beneath his, the taste of her was sweeter, more intoxicating than the finest wine he had ever drunk.

He could feel his control slipping, and only by the strength of his own will was he able to hold on to enough of his good sense to pull back from the temptation she offered. He had to remind himself of who she was and that he was only playing a role.

"Holly," he said in a low, husky voice, his eyes deepening to the shade of a stormy sea. Slowly, reluctantly, he released her, fighting to maintain some semblance of control while he still could. "I'd better try that call again," he muttered, forcing himself to turn around and walk out of the room, away from her.

Gripping the edge of the counter once again, Holly closed her eyes, taking deep ragged breaths in an effort to calm her turbulent emotions. This would never do. She sighed in desperation. He was right, it had been a foolhardy thing for her to do, placing an ad in the paper like that. She had left herself wide open to every creep in the city. Lucky for her David Winslow had happened along.

Or was it?

David called her unique, but that word fit him, as well. He was warm, gentle and compassionate, yet strong and masculine without the macho facade so many men found necessary to hide behind. The glimpses she'd had of his vulnerability only added to his appeal. He was a man who knew who he was and felt comfortable with himself. Also, it was rare to meet a man so unaware of the small pleasures of life. It was as though David had been sheltered from everyday things like shopping malls and video games. He was like someone who had been locked away in a prison.

Holly slumped against the counter. Good grief! Where had that ridiculous thought come from?

She stared at the intricate design of the tiled floor beneath her feet, battling to shove the troublesome thought aside. She turned her thoughts instead to the kiss they had just shared. It had been a gentle kiss, but she had sensed the fiery passion and hunger lurking beneath the surface of David's control. What would happen to her if all that latent passion was unleashed?

A scratching at the back door brought Holly back to the present and she drew in a long, deep breath. The dilemma of David was momentarily pushed aside as she went to let the cats in. She opened the door and stood aside to allow the two royal highnesses entrance. A fist on one hip, Holly observed the two furry felines with a wry smile. Cats were such regal, independent creatures, and these acted for all the world as though they owned this house and allowed her to stay only at their sufferance.

After closing the door, Holly leaned against it. "So, where have you guys been, out entertaining the ladies?"

All she got for her interest was a haughty glare from each of the tomcats as they strolled, heads high, to their bowls and calmly began eating.

"Excuse me for asking," Holly muttered, going to the cabinet to take down two mugs and fill them with coffee. "You know you're lucky to have me."

Puck, the Siamese, shot her a baleful glare while Calico ignored her completely.

"So much for gratitude!" She glared back at Puck. "See what happens the next time you come home from battling with that poodle down the street. You can fend for your independent self then and see how you like it." Picking up the mugs of coffee, she stalked away. Sometimes those darn cats made her feel like an intruder in her own kitchen.

The minute she stepped into the living room, all thoughts fled, and she was aware only of David's presence. Seeing him standing across the room from her, she was swamped again by the tangle of emotions he aroused in her. The doubts and questions assailed her at the same time as the thought that it seemed so very natural to see him there.

He turned to her then, the corner of his mouth lifting in a smile. "Do you always do that?"

"Do what?" she asked in confusion as he moved toward her.

Reaching for the mug she held out to him, David nodded toward the kitchen. "Do you always talk to yourself?" His work-roughened fingers lightly brushed hers as he wrapped his hand around the coffee mug.

Just the slight touch of his fingers had the power to unnerve her. Jerking her hand away, she avoided the probing intensity of his captivating eyes. Seating herself on the couch, she forced a lightness she was far from feeling. "I was arguing with the cats as usual. Self-centered little creatures."

David lowered his lean frame down beside her and chuckled. "Do they argue back?"

He was sitting so close his thigh rubbed against Holly's, raising her temperature by several degrees. "They have their ways. Do you want cream or sugar?"

"No, black is fine."

She lifted her own mug to her lips, her eyes drawn to the light sprinkling of fine black hairs across the back of his hand. He was turned slightly toward her, a sinewy forearm resting on his knee. Risking a glance at him, she was appalled at the sudden trembling in her hands when she found him studying her with unnerving intensity.

"Did you make your call?" Dragging her eyes from his, she leaned forward to set her mug on the coffee table before she embarrassed herself by spilling the hot liquid on her lap.

"They said the taxi would be about a half hour." Setting his mug down beside hers, he took her hand in his. "Holly, what's bothering you? Are you afraid of me?"

The sound of her name on his lips was like a caress, and any fear she felt came from within herself, from her almost-violent reaction to his touch, his nearness, his bold masculinity, but the nagging question of whether or not he had been in prison would not let go. How could she find out what she wanted to know without making a complete fool of herself?

"Have you been in prison?" she blurted out, and could have bitten off her tongue the moment the words were out of her mouth. That was a great approach, Nichols, she derided herself, about as subtle as a ton of bricks.

David stared at her in stunned shock.

She felt the hot flush of embarrassment suffusing her cheeks. Closing her eyes, she whispered, "I'm sorry! That was a stupid thing to say, but I thought . . . I wondered why . . . why you . . ."

He released her hand, but only to grasp her chin with his strong fingers. "Look at me, Holly," he commanded gently.

He would be furious with her, she thought, and rightfully so. But when she forced her eyelids open to view his harsh features, it wasn't anger she saw there, it was regret, laced with a touch of wistfulness.

"The only prison I've been in, little one," he whispered huskily, "was one of my own making."

"What do you mean?"

Tenderly he stroked the corner of her mouth with his rough thumb. "When you're working eighteen to twenty hours a day, there isn't much time for recreation."

"All work and no play," she quoted in a low voice.

"Makes David a dull boy, right? Do you think I'm dull, Holly?"

She shook her head, drugged by the fiery touch of his hand on her skin, by the deep huskiness of his voice. "Not dull," she denied gently, "just repressed. All you need is someone to teach you how to relax and enjoy life." It was with great restraint that she kept from raising her hands to run her fingers through that silk black hair, to feel his lips on hers.

David gazed deep into her eyes. They made him think of warm maple syrup. "I didn't realize how much I had missed until tonight. I've never met anyone quite like you, Holly Nichols."

He knew it was pure insanity to touch her again, yet he couldn't seem to help himself. His hand slid to the nape of her neck and he drew her to him. "Teach me,

Holly," he whispered in a low, slightly rough voice. "Show me more of what I've been missing."

When his lips captured hers it was with a hungry passion that sent the blood rocketing through her veins. Her fingers tangled in the shaggy hair at his nape, the silken strands clinging with a sensuous life of their own. Coaxing her lips apart, David's tongue invaded her mouth as he pushed her backward to lie full-length on the couch. He covered her body with his. His kiss was hard and passionate, yet tender and seductive at the same time, and waves of pleasure washed over her as David's mouth moved on hers. Her entire body felt alive, tingling with anticipation as his hands slid down her sides and slipped around her back.

She wrapped her arms around his broad shoulders, arching into him as his kiss deepened and robbed her of her usual good sense. Somewhere deep in her subconscious she knew she should put a stop to this, but it felt so right to feel his lips on hers, to have his strong arms wrapped tightly around her.

Finally David lifted his head, raising up slightly to prop himself on one elbow as he gazed down at her flushed face. His other hand rested on the curve of her waist. "Do you have any idea how you've disrupted my quiet, well-ordered life?"

Acutely aware of the lean body still stretched over the length of her, Holly managed a grin. "Quiet and well-ordered, hah! Dull and boring, you mean."

"Funny," he chuckled. "I've always considered it quiet and well-ordered. Now I have a dippy lady—"

"Dippy lady?"

"—tell me I'm dull and boring," he went on, ignoring the affronted expression on her face.

"Do you really think I'm dippy?"

"For a fact," he teased huskily. "Dippy, provocative, suicidal, seductive and sexy as hell." He bent his head to drop light kisses on her eyelids, the tip of her nose, her chin.

"I'm not sexy," Holly stated in a low voice.

David started to laugh, then saw the look in her eyes and realized she was dead serious. Was that what her jerk of a husband had done to her? Gently he drew her closer, rubbing his lips softly over hers.

"Honey, you are the most sweetly packaged little bundle of dynamite I've ever encountered."

"How would you know? You've led such a sheltered life."

"It can't have been a total loss," he said with a chuckle, burying his face in the curve of her neck. "I can still recognize quality when I see it, even if it is a bit dippy."

"You'll have a crash course in dippy when you meet my family this weekend."

All thoughts of her family disappeared when David's mouth once again captured hers. She knew she should stop now, while she could still think, but that was her last coherent thought as she succumbed to the magic of his kiss. It had been so long since she had felt like a desirable woman, so long since she had allowed anyone to get close enough to hold her and love her as David was doing. Her starving body responded with a passion that would have shocked her had she been capable of rational thought.

David slipped his hands beneath her sweater, and his touch on her bare skin sent ripples of heat surging through her. Wanting the same freedom, Holly tugged at his shirt until it came free of his jeans and she was able to run her own hands over his smooth, warm skin. Muscles rippled beneath her fingers as she explored the broad expanse of his back. Her own body was tingling with new sensations as David's hands moved over her, touching, stroking, bringing her to a level of desire she had never experienced before, had not even known existed.

She heard bells ringing, but that was nonsense. Nobody really heard bells, did they?

Suddenly David pulled away from her, his breathing harsh and ragged. Struggling through the mist of desire enveloping her, Holly fought to understand what was happening.

"David, what is it?"

"Someone's at the door."

The door? "Who would be ringing the doorbell at this time of night?"

David stood and began buttoning his shirt. When had it come unbuttoned? Holly wondered in a daze.

"It must be the cab driver," David said. "I'd better go tell him I'll be out in a minute, before he short-circuits the doorbell."

Holly lay on the couch watching him, wondering how he could stand up and walk across the room when she was too weak to move. The muffled sound of voices reached her ears as she sat up slowly, still struggling to understand what had happened to her. David had strolled into her office a few short hours ago and promptly robbed her of every ounce of common sense she possessed. Where had her cool, analytical mind been a few short minutes ago when she'd succumbed to a virtual stranger's soft words and seductive kisses? Never mind that he didn't seem like a stranger to her.

Mortified by her response to David's sensuous seduction, she repaired her disarranged clothes with shaking fingers. She couldn't allow this to happen again. It was important for her to keep this on a strictly business level. In three days David would be out of her life forever. Casual affairs were not her style.

She turned at the sound of the front door closing, taking a deep breath to prepare herself for seeing him again. He picked up his jacket and slipped it on as he entered the living room. Emerald eyes searched hers intently. "I'll see you tomorrow, Holly," he said softly, coming to stand too close to her for her comfort.

"The . . . the contract!" she stammered. "I haven't shown it to you yet."

His eyes narrowed slightly. "I can take it with me and give it to you tomorrow, if it's still important to you."

"Oh, it is," she insisted. She could feel his eyes on her as she snatched up her purse and dug the papers out to hand to him.

"Back to business, are we?" David's mouth twitched in amusement as he tucked the papers in his pocket without so much as glancing at them. He reached for her.

Holly tried to duck away, but he was too quick for her. Before she could protest, his mouth covered hers in a brief, hard kiss. "We'll stick to our little business arrangement for the weekend, darlin'," he whispered huskily, "but don't think you're going to get rid of me easily." With another brief kiss he released her and was gone.

HOLLY HATED waiting until the last minute. Wouldn't it be ironic if, after all she had gone through, she couldn't get reservations? Propping the telephone receiver on her shoulder, she opened the file on her desk, nervously tapping the edge with a pencil.

"I'm sorry, ma'am, but there are no seats available on that flight."

Gritting her teeth in frustration, Holly closed her eyes. "How about to Omaha?"

"Is that for this morning?"

"Yes." It would do no good to snarl, she decided, even though she had already told the woman several times that she needed the reservations for this morning. Hadn't her mother always told her she could get more with honey than with vinegar. She would be nice and hold her temper, even if it killed her.

"Ma'am? We have two seats on the eleven o'clock flight to Omaha."

Holly breathed a sigh of relief. "I'll take them."

"Fine. You will need to be at the airport an hour prior to flight time. Pick up your tickets at the airline ticket counter."

Where else would she pick them up? Holly wondered. "Thank you for all your help," she said sweetly. Showing remarkable self-control, she carefully replaced the receiver in its cradle.

Turning her attention to the file in front of her, she tried not to look at the clock and tried not to think

about last night. It was impossible, and frustrating.
There were several things she needed to clear up before
David arrived, but her brain had evidently atrophied.
She had been at the office since six-thirty, after spend-
ing a restless night tossing and turning, haunted by
teasing green eyes and seductive lips.

Holly tried to work, making a notation here, an ad-
justment there, her finely arched brows drawn together in concentration. Finally, she scrawled a note,
closed the file and clipped the note to the outside of the
folder. She needed to have Susan set up an appointment with the client sometime the following week.
Normally, Holly took great pleasure in working on Beatrice Armistead's account, for the woman was one of
her favorite clients, but this morning she had too many
other things on her mind.

Leaning back in her chair with a sigh, Holly wondered if she should forget about taking David with her.
Maybe she would be better off to pay him the money
when he arrived and send him on his way. She didn't
seem to have a lot of good sense where he was concerned.

"Good morning, Holly."

Holly flashed a welcoming smile at Susan. The tall
blonde looked stunning, as usual, in a charcoal-colored
suit and soft silk blouse in shades of silver gray and
charcoal. She envied Susan's ability to wear black with
such flair. If *she* wore black, she looked as if she were
ready to be laid out in a casket.

"You're looking chipper this morning," Holly said
with a smile. "Did Don Johnson show up on your
doorstep last night?" Susan's addiction to the popular

police show and her infatuation with the handsome lead actor were well-known.

"Don't I wish!"

"Tough luck," Holly teased, thinking of the surprising way her own evening had turned out. "Why don't you get a cup of coffee and we'll go over some things before I leave."

An hour and several cups of coffee later, Holly closed the last file and sighed with relief. There were no doubts in her mind that everything she asked would be done. She and Susan worked well together, and Holly knew she could trust her to carry out her wishes to the letter. Susan was the reason the office ran with such precision.

"Well, are you going to tell me about your appointment last night? Did you succeed in finding yourself a suitable fiancé?"

"You might say that," Holly muttered noncommittally, picking up her purse and checking for the tenth time to make sure she had her credit cards and anything else she might need for the trip. She knew Susan was dying of curiosity. For years she had been urging Holly to date, but Holly wasn't the least bit interested. Susan was the only person who knew the entire story of Holly's marriage and its aftermath.

Setting her coffee cup down on the desk, Susan said, "Is that all, Nichols?"

Holly looked up with what she hoped was a properly casual expression. "All? What more could you want?"

Resting her hands on the edge of the desk and leaning forward with a conspiratorial gleam in her gray eyes, Susan whispered, "I want every glorious, juicy little detail."

"Really, Susan!" Holly exclaimed, ducking her head so Susan couldn't see the slow flush on her cheeks. "There aren't any 'glorious, juicy' details!"

"Liar!"

Holly lifted her head, exposing the telltale red staining her cheeks. She knew that all the confusion she was experiencing from her meeting with David was showing on her face, but she couldn't help it. It did no good to try to hide anything from Susan, anyway. Susan knew her better than anyone.

Susan took one look at Holly and dropped onto the chair by Holly's desk. She studied her closely, noting every nuance of expression flickering across her face, then said gently, "Do you want to talk about it?"

Tossing her pencil onto the desk, Holly sighed in despair. "There isn't much to tell." She stood up and paced restlessly back and forth. "His name is David, but you already know that. He's about six feet tall, black hair, green eyes—"

"Devastatingly handsome?"

Holly thought for a moment, then shook her head. "Not really, but attractive in a rough sort of way. I took him home and introduced him to Brewster. Then we went to McDonald's, walked around the mall for a while, visited the arcade, and then I went home."

She stopped at the window for a moment to gaze out at the heavy morning traffic. When she once again turned around to face Susan, her expression was solemn and thoughtful. "He hadn't been to McDonald's in years, had never played a video game in his life and didn't even know what an Orange Julius was." She closed her eyes, remembering. "I asked him if he had been in prison."

Susan drew in her breath in a soft gasp. "What did he say?"

"He said no, of course." She was reluctant to elaborate on that part of the conversation, even with Susan. It was far too personal, along with a lot of other things that had happened between herself and David.

"He beat me at Pac-Man!"

Susan began to laugh and Holly glared at her. "It wasn't funny, Susan. My ego took a terrible beating."

"I can imagine! Come on, tell me more!"

"I told him about my family."

"And that didn't scare him off?"

Holly shook her head. "His is just as big. He has four brothers and two sisters, but he didn't tell me anything about them. He did tell me that his parents are dead." She paused for a moment. "I'd be willing to bet his family is nothing like mine," she went on. "He told me I was crazy to have run that ad, that I was lucky he wasn't some weird pervert. He liked my house, by the way," she declared smugly. "And he told me I'm unique."

"What did he say about your driving?"

"A lot! And none of it was kind! He accused me of signing a suicide pact with my car." She resumed her nervous pacing.

Susan nodded her head. "Sounds like an intelligent, levelheaded man to me." She studied her friend intently, her gray eyes sharp and perceptive. "Anything else?"

Holly came to a stop between Susan and the door. "Yes, he called me dippy!"

She watched Susan's eyes widen in surprise just as she heard a deep, husky chuckle from behind her. Strong hands settled on her shoulders, turning her around to face David's amused features. "Good morning, dippy lady," he teased, dropping a soft kiss on her startled lips.

"You . . . you're early," she stammered, struck nearly mute by his sudden appearance.

"No, I'm not," he replied, lifting his arm to glance at his watch. "I'm right on time."

"Oh," she said faintly. "I didn't realize it was so late." Marshaling her defenses, she stepped away from David to introduce him to Susan, certain that she could handle the exchange coherently if she put a safe distance between them.

Susan shook hands with David after shooting Holly a you-didn't-tell-me *everything* look. But Holly was too busy trying to retain a semblance of intelligence to notice. She had hoped seeing him again would calm some of the turbulence he'd caused last night. Broad daylight and all that rot! Instead, he looked even more appealing today. In fact, he looked magnificent with his unruly black hair and devastating green eyes, his lean, beautiful body clad in Levi's that left nothing to the imagination and a white knit shirt that set off his sun bronzed skin to perfection. *One look, one touch*, she thought, *and my brain goes to mush*. So much for sticking to business!

"Are you sure you're up to a whole weekend with this dippy lady?" Susan asked, grinning broadly at David.

"As long as I can keep her from behind the wheel of the car, I just might survive."

"What about from Omaha to Valentine?"

"That's easy," he replied in a firm voice. "I'm driving."

"Who said?" Holly interjected, indignation flashing in her eyes.

"I did." David dared her to dispute him.

"I've made that trip lots of times and managed to survive."

"Then I'd say the odds are dwindling."

"The way you drive it'll be midnight before we get there!"

David's eyes flashed wickedly. "Maybe later than that if we get lucky and run out of gas on some deserted road."

"That's what you think, Buster! We won't be traveling on any deserted roads unless you manage to get us lost." Holly hoped the Lord would forgive her for that little fib. David would find out soon enough that once you left the cities and interstates, every road in Nebraska could be designated as deserted.

"If we get lost, it won't be by accident. Are you ready to go?" he said, before she wasted any more time arguing with him. "The cab is waiting, so if you'll point me to your luggage, I'll take it out."

Holly motioned to where her two small pieces of luggage sat just inside the door. "Thank you," she murmured with a docile smile. Let him think for now that he had won this argument. "I have a couple of things to finish up with Susan, so I'll be out in a few minutes."

David held out his hand to Susan. "It's been a real pleasure, Susan. If I'm still walking, breathing and talking coherently, I'll see you when I get back."

"Good luck, David," she said with a grin. "She's really not so bad. She just requires a lot of patience."

"I'm a very patient man." Releasing her hand, he walked over to Holly's luggage, picked it up and strode from the room.

Holly turned to Susan with a warning glint in her eyes. "Don't say a word, Susan Martin! Not one word, do you hear?"

Susan held up her hands in mock defense. "I wasn't going to." Her eyes sparkled with mirth. "Well, maybe one or two."

"I gave you the key to my house, and Brewster is at the kennel. You know where the cat food is. Is there anything else?"

Susan shook her head. "Go on, get out of here! Don't worry about a thing. Just go have a good time with that gorgeous man you found. He almost makes me want to run an ad in the paper!"

Holly gave Susan an affectionate hug. "See you Monday. Wish me luck."

"I think you're going to need it."

4

DAVID LEANED BACK in his seat, wondering what the weekend would bring. It had been a long time since he had really looked forward to anything, but he was certainly looking forward to the next few days. He watched Holly as she peered out the window, marveling at how she found so much joy in life. She seemed to reach out and grab it with both hands—just as she had reached out and grabbed his heart.

Forcing such thoughts away, David reached for the flight magazine, but after reading a few pages he knew it was no use. He couldn't keep his mind on anything for very long. Meeting Holly had been quite an experience. He had spent a long, sleepless night tossing and turning because of her. The sound of her laughter had taunted him until dawn while the taste of her lingered in his memory. He hadn't been so frustrated since he was fifteen and discovered girls were remarkably different from boys.

David tilted his head back against the seat and closed his eyes, thinking that it had been an eternity since he was fifteen. He still remembered the frustration, though. Hadn't he just spent a long night trying to overcome it? Damn, but H. C. Nichols had managed to wreak havoc in his life! In a little more than twelve hours she had managed to turn it upside down. How was he going to keep his hands off her for the next two days? Damn that stupid contract! He had read it last night, and though it was as full of holes as Swiss cheese, he would try to abide by it for Holly's sake. After all, they would be staying at her parents' house and he had more sense than to upset any woman's father, even if the woman happened to be a mature businessperson in her twenties.

Settling deeper into the seat, David began to relax. Holly hadn't been the only thing on his mind last night. He had spent a great deal of time thinking about this weekend and his reasons for going; about Nick; about the threat of a court injunction; about the civic center and all its problems; and, finally, about what he wanted to do with the rest of his life.

A wave of weariness washed over him, and he knew it wasn't caused solely by one sleepless night. The years of work and responsibility weighed on him, making him feel twice his age.

So many questions, he thought tiredly, and so few answers. Despite his lofty reasoning, he knew deceiving Holly was wrong. Somehow he would find a way to make it up to her, but for the next three days he intended to do something he had never done before— something those closest to him would never believe him capable of doing. He was going to ignore the rest of the world, including his business, the civic center, his family and every other responsibility he had carried for half his life. The next couple of days were for him, David Winslow Branson. The rest would be there waiting for him on Monday morning.

John was appalled when David told him he would be incommunicado for three days. When questioned, David merely said he was going away, and refused to offer anything more.

Now there was nothing to do but relax, to take time for himself and explore all the new and disturbing emotions H. C. Nichols had awakened in him. One thing was certain—it wouldn't be boring.

Holly watched the vast sprawl of Indianapolis fall away below her, then settled back in her seat, trying to keep her mounting excitement under control. She looked forward to the weekend and spending time with her family, but a quick glance at the man seated next to her made Holly admit that David's presence added extra excitement to this particular trip.

She turned from the window to gaze at him. Sooty lashes lay across the curve of his cheekbones. The unruly ebony hair tumbling around his face made him look young and vulnerable. How was she going to keep her hands off him for an entire weekend? But he had signed that dumb contract and given it back to her during the drive to the airport. She had a gut feeling he intended to abide by it to the letter.

Her lips curved in a smile at the memory of the kisses he'd rained on her in the taxi. The way he put it, he was storing up for the long dry spell. How could you fault that kind of logic?

Shifting to a more comfortable position, Holly leaned her head back and closed her eyes. She hadn't slept much after David left and the long, restless night was catching up with her. Her head rolled slowly over to rest on David's shoulder and she drifted off to sleep.

THE NEXT THING Holly knew, someone was shaking her and a deep voice rumbled in her ear. Mumbling something suitably obscene and incoherent, she burrowed deeper into the warm, firm pillow.

"Holly, wake up!" the voice persisted. "Come on, wake up."

Hovering on the edge of slumber, she fought waking up with a stubbornness born from long years of practice. "Go 'way," she muttered. "Don't wanna get up."

Fighting the urge to laugh, David ignored her petulance and shook her gently. "Do you want me to throw you over my shoulder and carry you off the plane?"

Groggily Holly forced her eyes open, disoriented from being awakened from a sound sleep. "Plane? What plane? Where are we?"

"Omaha."

Reality rushed in with a vengeance. The subtle scent of David's woodsy after-shave was much too vivid for comfort, as was the warmth penetrating the entire side of her face. With a start, she realized her face was burrowed in the curve of his shoulder. Flushing scarlet, Holly jerked upright, averting her face while smothering a yawn.

She decided to play it casual, not give him an opening to say one word about her sleeping on his shoulder for the past few hours.

"Omaha! Already?" She leaned over to look out the window. "What happened to lunch?"

David rolled his eyes. "I might have known."

Holly shot him a scathing look. "What does that mean?"

"Are you always this grumpy when you miss a meal?" he asked.

"I'm not grumpy," she grumbled, glancing past David to the other passengers filing down the center aisle. She reached under the seat to retrieve her carry-on bag and her purse. After adjusting the straps over her shoulder, she glared at him. "Well? Are you going to just sit there?"

David leaned toward her, his eyes glittering with wicked humor. "If I promise to feed you, will you smile?"

Biting her lip to keep from doing just that, Holly struggled to keep a straight face. How could she stay in a rotten mood when just looking at him gave her a warm glow? David couldn't help it if she was a snarler when she woke up. "How much is it worth to you?" she managed to say.

"Two all-beef patties, special sauce, lettuce—"

Holly sputtered helplessly, pressing her fingers to her mouth in a desperate attempt to keep from laughing.

"—cheese, pickles, onions—"

Collapsing into gales of laughter, Holly fell back on the seat, her eyes brimming with tears.

"—on a sesame seed bun!" he finished triumphantly, then glared at her in mock seriousness. "You're making a spectacle of yourself, Holly. People are staring." Merriment danced in his emerald eyes. "Do you know how long it took me to memorize all that?" He didn't even know where it had come from. The old commercial had popped into his head from nowhere.

"You did good. I always got my tongue tangled around the special sauce, lettuth, cheeth—" Holly was interrupted by another fit of giggles. "Thee?"

Laughter rumbled from deep in David's chest. "Do you know you are certifiably nutso!" Grasping her by the waist he lifted her out of the seat and stood her in the aisle. "Now, not only do I have to feed you, I have to untangle your tongue. How will it look if I deliver you to your mother talking like Elmer Fudd?"

The teasing banter continued as they left the plane and waited for their luggage at the carousel. An hour later they were settled into the small economy car Holly rented, heading toward Highway 275, the route to Valentine.

"Where would be a good place to eat lunch, Holly?" David asked as they were leaving the city behind.

"I don't know. We should keep it light, though. Mom will have a huge dinner fixed when we get there. By the way, my culinary tastes include more than fast food."

"Oh, really? Like what, for instance?"

"Just about everything from apples to zucchini."

"Well, that narrows it down," he stated with a laugh. "There's a truck stop up ahead. How does that sound?"

"Fine," Holly agreed, her eyes drawn to his strong hands on the steering wheel. The more she got to know David Winslow, the more time she spent with him, the more bewildered she became by how he'd come to be here.

"David?"

"Hmm?

"Why did you answer that ad I put in the paper?"

David didn't reply right away, not until he'd guided the car into the parking lot of the truck stop and shut off the engine. He ran his hand through his hair, then turned to face her, draping one arm across the back of the seat.

"Does it really matter, Holly?"

She searched his rough features. "Yes, I think it does."

"Why?"

Knotting her hands together in her lap, Holly looked past him to the line of eighteen-wheelers parked across from them—anything to avoid being drawn into the depths of David's sea-green eyes. "You don't seem the type to even read the personal column, let alone answer one of the ads."

David thought long and hard, knowing his answer would be crucial. Now was definitely not the time to tell her the truth. "Holly, I can honestly say I have never answered one of those ads before in my life."

"Then why did you this time?" She swung her gaze back to him in time to see the sooty lashes sweep downward.

"I guess you could say I was coerced into it," he said at last.

"You mean, someone set you up?" Her eyes were shadowed with doubt.

"You could say that."

"Are you sorry?"

His gaze softened as he reached out to touch her cheek. "I've never been less sorry about anything in my life."

Holly felt like shouting as a swift rush of pleasure swept through her. "Even if I'm nutso and dippy?"

David gave a low laugh. "I wouldn't have you any other way." Sliding his hand upward across her jawline, he slipped his fingers into her short curly hair. Gently he nudged her toward him, then stopped, releasing her with a frustrated sigh. "Damn that stupid contract!" Flicking her a rueful glance, he said, "Come on, my little nutso, dippy lady. Let's get something to eat and hit the road."

"HAVE YOU driven this all alone?"

Holly shook her head. "I usually fly into Grand Island, which is a lot closer to Valentine, but the airline's schedule just didn't fit mine this time."

"How big is Valentine?" David asked.

"About twenty-six-hundred people. It's a nice town, a lot different mode of living than Indianapolis. The busiest time of the year, other than harvest, is February. People from all over the country send their Valentines to be postmarked there."

David rubbed his chin thoughtfully. "Do you realize there are apartment complexes in Indianapolis that house more people than comprise the entire town of Valentine?"

Holly gave a derisive snort. "Disgusting, isn't it? A lot of people suggested I live in one of those condominium complexes, simply because the upkeep on a house takes so much more time and effort. But I like working in the yard and having space around me. Wall-to-wall people doesn't appeal to me." She slid down in the seat and propped a knee against the dashboard.

David looked over at her and smiled indulgently. "Comfortable?"

"Yep!" Holly flashed him a teasing grin. "Are you nervous about meeting my family?"

"Should I be?" When she shrugged, he chuckled softly. "Ask me again around midnight."

"Tell me about your brothers and sisters, David," she said.

David shifted in his seat. "They aren't like your family, Holly," he said evasively.

"That doesn't tell me a thing," she stated with a hint of laughter in her voice. "There aren't many families like mine."

"We don't have any race-car drivers or interstate truck drivers." At her pointed glare, David knew he couldn't stall her for long. He sighed in resignation. "My brother Gary is a captain in the air force. He's a fighter pilot, stationed at Nellis Air Force Base outside Las Vegas. He got married a couple of years ago and he and his wife have a little boy, Jeremy, who is six months old."

"A fighter pilot, huh?" Holly's eyes twinkled merrily. "Right, David! That isn't nearly as daring as a race-car driver or a trucker. Is he older or younger than you?"

"Younger. All of them are younger. I'm the old man of the family. After Gary is Tom. He's a stockbroker and lives in New York. Tom isn't married."

"No wonder," Holly retorted. "Who would want to marry a stuffy old stockbroker!"

"Tom isn't stuffy, just quiet and refined."

"As in dull and boring?" She looked over at him and smiled innocently.

David gave an exaggerated sigh. "I thought you wanted to hear about my family."

"Sorry," she said with an unrepentant grin. "I'll try to behave."

"After Tom is Robert. He just graduated from law school and joined a large firm in Chicago." David kept his eyes on the road, ignoring her smothered exclamation. "My sister Cheryl is married and has two children, a boy and a girl."

When David was silent for several moments, Holly gave him a questioning glare. "Well?"

"Well, what?"

"Who is Cheryl married to," she prodded, "a senator or something?"

David shot her a warning glance. "A doctor," he snapped. "Are you satisfied?"

Her face was a mask of innocence. "I wasn't going to say a word."

"I'll bet! Well, you can relax. Kate is an artist and runs a gallery in Santa Fe."

Holly rolled her eyes. She couldn't even draw a stick figure and she was supposed to be unimpressed by someone who was obviously a successful artist? "So that makes her a rebel? Good Lord, David, you have a doctor, a lawyer and an Indian ch . . . a stockbroker! What more could one family ask for?"

"How about a little respect! I didn't make one improper remark about your family."

"That's because you were wandering around in a daze somewhere between Denver and Omaha." At his warning glance, Holly sat up in the seat and arranged her features into what she hoped was a proper expression of respect.

"Well, that takes care of all but one," she said after a long pause. "I can't wait to hear about him!"

David's eyes shadowed with sudden despair. "Nick is the next to youngest. It took me two years to talk him into going to college, then he decided to drop out after a few weeks last fall."

Holly gauged the dark expression on David's face, noting the grim set of his jaw and the faint tightness around his mouth. "Where is he now?" she asked softly.

"I don't know," he finally admitted. "He calls once in a while to let me know he's still alive."

She bit back the questions she longed to ask, knowing instinctively that he did not want to be pressed about Nick. Instead she said, "So how did you end up in construction work in the middle of all those doctors and lawyers? Are you a bit of a rebel, too?"

David looked out the window at the miles of rolling grassland, his forehead furrowed in a frown. "Does the kind of work I do bother you?"

"Of course not!" Holly retorted. "Really, David, I'd be much more intimidated if you were a doctor or lawyer!"

He couldn't resist laughing. "I can't imagine you being intimidated by anyone, Holly." Gesturing toward a spot somewhere ahead of them, he took his foot off the accelerator to slow the car. "Do you want to stop at that roadside park up ahead and stretch your legs for a few minutes?" He was amazed at the deftness at which he had evaded Holly's question.

"Sounds good to me. We'll be in Valentine in an hour or so. We would have been there by now if I'd been driving." The last words were muttered under her breath.

"I heard that," David retorted, braking for the turn into the park. He parked the car and climbed out, stretching his lean body and sighing softly, then he gazed at her over the top of the car. "Tell me what's on the agenda for the weekend."

Holly met him in front of the car, her eyes raking his six-foot frame hungrily. Just the sight of him sent a tingle up and down her spine. Since leaving Omaha, she'd almost had to sit on her hands to keep them from touching him. A slight breeze ruffled his dark hair and Holly remembered how it had felt to run her fingers through its luxuriant thickness. Cold showers would definitely be on the agenda, she thought. How many could she take without her parents getting suspicious?

"Holly, if you don't quit looking at me like that, I'm going to forget all about that damned contract!"

She looked up and inhaled swiftly, the naked yearning in his eyes making her knees weak. *Take the contract*, she begged silently. *Burn it, rip it up, blow it away, pulverize it. See if I care.*

Whirling away from him, Holly walked toward a cluster of pine, oak and maple trees. Several picnic tables in various stages of disrepair were scattered around the small clearing. A bed of pine needles muffled her steps as she tried to remember what David had asked her. Something about the weekend. Oh, yes—the agenda.

"Tomorrow there'll be a big picnic in the park. Mom and Dad have all sorts of games and activities planned for everyone. How are you at touch football?" She dared a glance at him, aware of the tremor in her voice. Would he notice and, if he did, would he know the reason for it?

He noticed and understood. It didn't make it any easier to know she was fighting the same battle as he. It took all his willpower not to take her in his arms. "Is it going to be coed?"

Holly forced a scowl, ignoring the fire still burning in his eyes. "I'm talking about touch football, David, not tackle!"

Taking a step toward her, David attempting a slight smile. "I'd settle for a touch at this point," he said softly.

Her defenses were weakening rapidly. Why did he have to be so damnably attractive? Dropping her gaze from his, she managed to go on. "Tomorrow night is the anniversary party. First we'll all go to Michael's church, where Mom and Dad will renew their vows, then Michael will give a short talk. Afterward, it's back to the house for cake and homemade ice cream and partying until the wee hours." There would be dancing, too, she thought, giving her a chance to be in David's arms for at least part of the time. "Does it sound terribly homespun and boring, David?"

Perching his lean frame on the edge of a picnic table, David smiled gently. "No, Holly, it sounds very nice, very family, and I'm looking forward to it." He gazed at her for a long, sensual moment, then held out his hand. "Come here, Holly," he commanded softly.

She thought in despair that if he didn't want her to ravish his body right here in this roadside park, he shouldn't ask her to touch him. When she didn't move, he stood up and went to her. Grasping her hand gently but firmly, he guided her to the table and sat her down on the bench. It was a good thing, because her legs suddenly felt like limp spaghetti.

"There's one thing missing from this engagement idea of yours," he said. "Do you know what it is?"

She wished it was that stupid contract, but she had a feeling it was her common sense. Pushing a strand of hair back from her face, she shook her head. "I thought I'd covered everything."

Digging in his pocket, David extracted something and held it in front of her shocked eyes. It was a ring, and not just any ring but a lovely sapphire surrounded by sparkling diamonds.

"Where on earth did you get something like that?" she gasped.

There was a shuttered look to his face as he reached for her hand and slipped the ring on her finger. The ring had belonged to his mother. "I borrowed it from a friend. We can't have you going home with a fiancé and no ring."

She stared at the ring in disbelief. "That must be some friend."

She had caught him there. "It belongs to my sister," he stated softly, hating the addition of still another lie. "The doctor's wife."

Holly looked up at him with something akin to terror in her eyes. "Oh, David, I can't wear this! What if I lose it?" She could picture herself working for the next ten years to pay for it.

"It won't get lost," David assured her with a grin. "I intend to be right there at your side every minute, guarding it with my life."

Jumping up from the bench, Holly paced back and forth, unable to drag her eyes from the lovely ring. She didn't know what had stunned her the most: the ring or the fact that David had thought of it.

As she turned back to him, Holly's heart lurched in her chest. David leaned against the table, his dark-fringed eyes studying her intently. Gathering her courage, she walked toward him, her eyes locked with his.

"Thank you, David," she said, coming to a halt in front of him. "That was very sweet of you."

"Sweet had nothing to do with it," he said with a slow smile that could probably melt steel. "I was protecting myself. How was I to explain to your brother why you didn't have a ring?"

Holly looked down at the sparkling ring on her finger and chuckled. "They're all going to think you're filthy rich."

David's features took on an almost-somber expression as he gazed down at her. "Well, when you tell Michael this whole thing was a joke, you can always tell him the ring was, too."

Holly took a step closer, wondering at the sudden wariness in David's eyes and the almost rigid stance of his lean body. "David, would you do me a favor?" she asked in a voice that was low and husky.

The wariness in his eyes deepened. "That depends on what it is."

She placed her hands on his shoulders, feeling the warmth of his skin beneath the smooth cotton knit of his shirt. There was a smile on her lips as she moved even closer. "Would you forget that contract for a minute and kiss me?"

The look in her eyes held an invitation he hadn't the power to resist. "You bet I will!" he moaned gratefully, reaching out to drag her into his arms.

A soft sigh escaped her when at last David's lips captured hers. It had been so long, she thought, her arms moving of their own accord to circle his neck. His kiss was urgent, hungry, coaxing. Holly leaned into him, conscious of how perfectly they fitted together. His tongue invaded her mouth, sending lightening flashes of sensual pleasure rocketing through her veins. She raked her fingers through the silky strands of his hair, giving herself up to the magic of being in his arms again. His mouth moved over hers, devouring its softness. He was like a starving man at a banquet table. When he finally lifted his mouth from hers, her body felt heavy and warm.

"Is my minute up yet?" he murmured against her lips.

"Who's counting?" she managed to say, kissing the corner of his mouth, then his chin, before moving back to the inviting softness of his lips.

He took command, caressing her lips more than actually kissing them, rubbing back and forth until Holly was weak with wanting. Too soon he raised his head to emit a long, shuddering breath. Gathering her close, he held her gently until their breathing returned to a semblance of normalcy. "We'd better go before I have to explain to your folks why we're late for dinner." Gazing down into her smoldering eyes, he brushed her eyelids closed with a featherlike kiss. "You're a very special lady, Holly Nichols. When this contract expires, we're going to have to renegotiate some of the more ridiculous stipulations it happens to contain."

Holly nodded mutely. Despite everything, she had to admit it would be very easy to fall in love with a man like David.

5

DAVID SLOWED the car as they entered Valentine from the east. Main street rolled through the center of town, flanked on either side by the numerous stores and businesses found in every small town in America. There was an old brick courthouse and post office, both used for other purposes now that they had been replaced by newer, more modern facilities in the name of progress. The silvery surface of the water tower looming in the distance gleamed in the slanting rays of the lowering sun. Holly's roots were here in the sand hills of Nebraska and she couldn't contain the rush of anticipation at the thought of being reunited with all the people she held dear.

"Well, this is it." Holly eyed David with a trace of trepidation. What was he thinking as he took in the sights of downtown Valentine, Nebraska?

His eyes mirrored pleasure when he turned his head and winked at her. "It looks as if it's been sitting here, just like this, for a hundred years."

"Close, very close, Mr. Big-City Person. I'm not quite sure how long the town has been here, but Cherry County celebrated its centennial a couple of years ago."

As they approached the west end of town, David gazed around with interest. He envied Holly her roots. He hadn't had any real roots in years.

Holly was almost bouncing up and down in anticipation, her eyes dancing. David found it difficult to concentrate on his driving. How long was it since he had been that excited about anything?

A few minutes later she pointed to a gravel road a short distance ahead and to their left. "There's the road to the house."

Holly moved to the edge of her seat when the road curved around to reveal a huge, rambling frame house with a wide porch wrapped around two sides. She was so excited she didn't hear David's soft intake of breath. An assortment of cars filled the long driveway and David pulled up behind a midsize station wagon bearing Colorado license plates and switched off the engine.

The hum of the motor had no sooner died away than the front door of the house swung open and a swarm of family descended on the new arrivals. Holly was out of the car in a flash, immediately surrounded by a horde of laughing, shouting brothers and sisters.

David climbed out of the car and propped an arm on the roof, watching the entire spectacle with an amused smile. It was impossible to sort out who was who in the confused jumble, but he spotted Holly's mother immediately. Ellen Nichols was an older, more mature version of her off-beat daughter. And the big, barrel-chested, graying man standing back and observing the melee with an expression of patient tolerance could be none other than Sam Nichols, patriarch of the clan. Sam turned his head and caught David's eye, his piercing gaze silently appraising the younger man. David lifted his shoulders and threw up his hands in a gesture of total confusion. Sam's broad, weather-lined face split in a wide smile.

Holly gazed at the familiar faces surrounding her as she was pulled into her mother's welcoming embrace.

"We were expecting you long before this," Ellen Nichols exclaimed, her eyes drifting to the dark-haired man on the other side of the car. "You've never been this late before."

David walked around the front of the car and moved to Holly's side, slipping an arm around her waist. "I guess that's my fault, Mrs. Nichols. I wouldn't allow Holly to drive." His green eyes danced with mischief.

"Ridden with her before, have you?" Ellen gazed up at the attractive man who held Holly so possessively, her brown eyes sparkling with curiosity.

"Yes, ma'am," David replied solemnly. "The menace of Valentine has become the menace of Indianapolis, but I intend to change all that." He didn't bat an eye when Holly's elbow dug into his ribs.

Ellen fought a grin. "Oh, you do, do you!"

All eyes were on David as he bent to whisper in Ellen's ear. Everyone was interested in this "friend" Holly had brought home with her. "Even if I have to turn her over my knee," David declared in a stage whisper.

Holly's face twisted into a black scowl amid a chorus of giggles and snickers. Ellen laughed, reaching up to plant a kiss on David's cheek.

"Welcome to the Nichols clan, David!" Turning to her daughter, Ellen said, "Holly Carol Nichols, I think you've met your match!"

Holly mumbled something about traitors and blood being thicker than water before she and David were engulfed in a flood of introductions. She had been worrying about how David would fit in with her family and it had taken him less than five minutes to be accepted with an ease that left her somewhat stunned.

Michael stepped forward, gave her a lopsided grin and said, "This is quite a surprise, Holly."

"How can it be such a surprise, Michael, when you announced it from the pulpit last month?"

"But—"

"David, this is my brother Michael. Michael, my fiancé, David Winslow."

The two shook hands while Holly looked on. She thoroughly enjoyed the confusion on her brother's face. David, bless him, carried the whole thing off with perfect aplomb. Holly fought the urge to applaud.

David's arm rested lightly around her waist as they moved away from Michael and the entire clan ambled up the sloping lawn to the house. Joe swung a squealing Amy onto his broad shoulders, ducking low to enter the front door. Bobby and Kevin chased each other across the rambling porch, a shaggy dog of indeterminate ancestry nipping at their heels.

At the bottom of the stairs, David pulled Holly to one side to avoid the crush. "How am I doing so far?" he whispered in her ear.

Holly tilted her head back to give him a saucy grin. "Aside from the fact that you have my entire family eating out of your hand, I'd say you're holding your own."

"It's my devastating charm," he declared with a smug grin. "Gets 'em every time."

A half hour later, Holly left David in the care of Joe and her brother-in-law Rob while she went to help with the preparations for dinner. Involved in a deep discussion about racing cars versus motorcycles, an endless topic of conversation when Joe and Rob got together, David probably wouldn't even notice she was gone, Holly decided as she entered the big warm kitchen.

The steady hum of conversation ceased abruptly as four pairs of eyes swiveled to rest on Holly. The masks of innocence worn by her sisters and mother were not lost on her.

"Did I interrupt something?" she asked warily, crossing the room to swipe a pickle from an assortment of jars on the big round oak table. It was one of her mother's homemade dills and Holly relished the flavor, observing the aborted dinner preparations with studied casualness. The huge kitchen was filled with the aroma of fried chicken and homemade yeast rolls. Louisa stood at the counter mashing potatoes, Ellen was stirring gravy, Brianny was chopping ingredients for coleslaw and Tina was arranging the relish tray.

At least that's what everyone had been doing prior to Holly's entrance. Now they were standing, spoon, ladle, knife and celery stick in hand, studying her with a dozen questions in their eyes.

Holly strolled to the stove and lifted a lid to investigate what was cooking. "Anything I can do to help?"

"Michael fell for it hook, line and sinker," her mother said with a smile. "I must admit, Holly, your friend is something!"

"How old is he?"

"Where did you meet him?"

"Has he ever been married?"

"Does he have a family?"

"Doesn't this tribe scare him at all?"

Leaning against the refrigerator, Holly seemed to be deep in concentration. "Thirty-four, you wouldn't believe it if I told you, no, yes, not so far." Shifting her gaze to each of her sisters in turn, then to her mother, Holly smiled innocently. "Any more questions?"

Louisa poured milk into the potatoes, chuckling as Brianny tossed a carrot stick at Holly. "He must be quite a friend to go along with this joke of yours. How did you meet him?" Lou was tall and willowy, with a cap of short dark hair and Sam's blue eyes.

I ran an ad. "I haven't known him very long," Holly admitted, "and I met him . . . through another friend." She dared not look at Brianny, the only one in the room besides herself who knew she had advertised for him, or she knew she would laugh. Holly took the long-handled spoon from her mother and began stirring the gravy.

Tina looked up from the relish tray where she was arranging a section of stuffed olives. "I guess you're going to tell us he isn't the least, tiny bit intimidated by this crazy family! And another thing. How come you've never mentioned such a friend before?"

Holly stepped to one side so her mother could reach a pot of green beans on the back burner. "He isn't. In fact, his family is bigger. He has four brothers and two sisters."

Just then the kitchen door swung open and Holly heaved a sigh of relief at being rescued from answering Tina's other question. A very pregnant Sandy entered, her face bearing the marks of sleep. "Sorry I wasn't up when you got here, Holly," she apologized, going over to give her sister-in-law a hug. "It seems all I do anymore is sleep."

Holly looked at Sandy's figure and grinned. "I guess I'll forgive you, under the circumstances."

Finally the scrumptious feast was ready. Holly's mouth watered as she helped dish up the food and carry it into the dining room. Dinner would be served buffet style, and while her mother went to announce that it was time to eat, Holly and Brianny finished arranging the silverware and napkins at one end of the long table.

"Holly, are you going to tell me that David is who you got when you ran an ad in the paper?"

Holly didn't look up. "It is hard to believe, isn't it?"

"Almost too good to be true," her sister murmured. "You'd better not let it get around. You could start a trend that might prove disastrous."

Holly thought of the others who had answered the ad and began to laugh. "I wouldn't recommend it to everyone," she said.

David came up behind her and slipped his arms around her waist. Blushing furiously when he bent his head to nuzzle her nape, she tried unsuccessfully to twist out of his grasp.

"Still needs a little taming, doesn't he?" Brianny quipped. "But, then again, so does she."

"I'm working on it," David chuckled, grunting when Holly elbowed him in the stomach.

"You've got your work cut out for you," Sam warned in his gravelly voice, patting David on the shoulder.

Holly glared up at her father. "Whose side are you on?"

Sam chucked Holly under the chin, then reached for a plate. "I'm on anyone's side who can take you in hand and keep you out of trouble." He looked at David with an expression of despair. "The terror of Valentine, she was. I hope you know what you're letting yourself in for."

"It's been a crash course in patience, sir."

Holly glared at the two of them, then stomped off to the kitchen to let them decide by themselves how best to "handle" her. It seemed her family was ganging up on her, determined to play their roles to the hilt.

Later, sitting cross-legged on the floor of the living room, Holly listened to the buzz of conversation around her. It was good to be home, to be sitting here with her family around her and David next to her. Rick had never felt at ease with her family, nor they with him. Yet David, a virtual stranger—heaven help her if her family found out how much of a stranger—seemed as much a part of them as Rob or Sandy. He acted as if he'd known them all for years. And wasn't that just how she felt about him? It had been a little more than twenty-four hours since he'd arrived at the door of her office, yet Holly was having difficulty remembering what her life had been like without his laughing eyes and husky voice.

Leaning toward her with a crispy golden-brown chicken thigh in his hand, David murmured, "Can you cook like this?"

Holly looked at him with an expression of disbelief on her face. "You've seen how I love to eat and you can ask a question like that?" Glancing at David's fast-disappearing second helping of food, she chuckled. "Enjoying yourself, city boy?" His shoulder brushed hers and she felt that now familiar rush of pleasure. Bold, thick-lashed eyes sought and held hers, a sensual message burning in their jade-green depths.

"I haven't had an appetite like this in years," he said softly, his gaze moving to rest on her parted lips.

The double meaning was not lost on her. She felt the heat clear to her core. "Wait till you taste Mom's apple pie," she said in a choked whisper. But *I'd rather have you for dessert* was the message she sent back with her eyes. One cold shower coming right up. She looked over at Michael, nearly laughing at the pensive expression on his face when she caught him staring at them. Holly knew he was still trying to figure out exactly what was going on.

"Anyone for pie?" Ellen stood up and scanned the moaning mass of people sprawled all over her living room.

"She's got to be kidding," David groaned, rolling his eyes in misery. "Is she trying to kill us with kindness?"

Ellen propped her hands on her still-slender waist. "Not a chance, David Winslow!" She looked over at Michael, than back to David. "I intend to make certain everyone here is alive and well long enough to see you married to that dippy daughter of mine!" She shook her head in perplexity as Holly and David looked at each other and collapsed into gales of laughter.

IT WAS JUST a few minutes past six the next morning when Holly, dressed in soft brushed-denim jeans, a bright turquoise pullover, sneakers and a lightweight nylon jacket, crept quietly downstairs. Everyone was still asleep, she thought, as she passed through the living room to the front door. Pausing with her hand on the knob, she feasted her eyes on the huge, silent living room. Funny, it didn't seem all that big when the family was gathered there. Deep-cushioned couches, overstuffed chairs, all covered in bright floral prints, were grouped invitingly around the room. Sam's favorite recliner sat in its place of honor near the full-wall stone fireplace. Needlework and craft pictures, along with photographs of every member of the family, graced the sand-colored walls. It was a warm and inviting room, despite its spacious size, and Holly had imitated Ellen's special taste in decorating her own home.

Holly opened the door and stepped out into the brisk, early-morning air. Inhaling deeply, she reveled in the beautiful spring day. The sun would burn away the chill in a few hours, and temperatures in the low seventies had been forecast by the local expert. Still, it was risky at best to plan an outdoor party this time of year in northern Nebraska. A blizzard, even this late in the season, was not impossible.

Stepping off the porch, she headed around the house toward the dense stand of trees bordering the creek that ran through the center of the property. She needed some time alone. Time to think about everything that had happened over the past couple of days, to sort out her feelings for David. She was confused and a bit undone by the way he filled her thoughts every waking minute. If she didn't know better, she would swear she was falling in love with him. And that would be the dumbest thing she had ever done in her life. No one fell in love in two days.

Walking deep into the woods along the creek path, she sighed in despair. This whole plan threatened to blow up in her face in the worst possible way. Her family was outspoken in its unanimous approval of David. Even Sam was taken with him. It wasn't all that easy to win Sam's approval. Rick had never accomplished it.

Shoving her hands into her pockets, Holly came to a halt. Leaning back against a giant elm tree, she stared at the water rippling and gurgling over its rocky bed. This had been a favorite spot of hers as a child. Just around the bend the creek widened and deepened to a pool ideal for swimming. She had done a lot of serious thinking here. It had been in this exact spot that she had decided to go home and file for a divorce a week after she'd walked into their sleek modern house and caught Rick in bed with another woman. She'd fled home to Valentine, shaken to the core but unable to talk about what had happened, even to her parents. Yet when she had told them of her decision to divorce Rick, they had given their love and support as they always did, while respecting her right to privacy.

Holly had gone back to Indianapolis and promptly moved out of the house she and Rick had shared during the two years of their marriage. Rick was furious. Some of the words he hurled at her still rang in her ears. She had wanted nothing from him but her freedom, and when the divorce was final, there was nothing to show for the years of their marriage but a lot of bad memories. She hadn't even kept his name.

Now she was back in this lovely spot, surrounded by tall pine, maple, elm and oak trees, serenaded by birds and the soft murmur of the creek, thinking about another man. David. What was she to do about him?

"Good morning."

Her breath caught in her throat and the blood leaped through her veins at the sound of his deep resonant voice. Was he really here or had she conjured him up from her daydreams? But no, there he was, no more than a foot in front of her, his ebony hair still damp from his shower, his lean body clad in form-fitting Levi's and the same dark blue windbreaker he had worn the night she met him.

"Hi," she greeted him, smiling instead of giving in to the desire to throw herself into his arms. "I see you're surviving the onslaught rather well."

The corners of his mouth curved in a smile. "I don't know if I am or not. How good are you at persuasion?"

"Need you even ask? I got you here, didn't I?"

"That you did," he conceded. "The question is, where do we go from here?" David came closer, propping his shoulder against the tree. "Holly, we've got a real problem," he said slowly. "I have two tickets to the Indy 500, an invitation to dinner with Joe the night before the race, an offer from Tim to join him at the Cheyenne Frontier Days in August, an open invitation to go skiing with Brianny and Alan in the Rockies next winter and an offer from Michael to perform our wedding ceremony."

"Is that all?" she asked weakly.

David shook his head.

"I didn't think so," she murmured.

"I thought it would do for starters." He pushed away from the tree and surveyed the wooded glade. "It's a beautiful morning."

Holly raked his broad back with her eyes, remembering the feel of those hard muscles beneath her fingertips. "David, this is serious," she said tightly.

Thrusting his hands into the back pockets of his Levi's, he ducked his head, not saying anything for a long moment. "I'm afraid it is, Holly," he said at last. Pivoting to face her, he devoured her with his eyes, taking in every detail of her small face and petite body. "More serious than you know," he muttered.

His words sent a tremor through her. "David..."

"Your mother is fixing breakfast," he said huskily. "We should get back."

Holly nodded mutely, leaving the solid support of the tree to fall into step beside David. He was pensive as they walked through the woods, his eyes distant. All she could think of was the easy grace of his movements, the strength of his leanly muscled body and the elusive scent of his after-shave.

They left the wooded area and started across the clearing toward the house. David stopped suddenly, slipping his arm around her waist and turning her into the circle of his arms. Before she could react, he bent his head and took her mouth in a slow, drugging kiss that threatened her equilibrium.

"David, what are you doing?" she gasped when his lips left hers to caress the curve of her cheek. She could see her mother moving around in the kitchen.

"This is for your mother," he whispered, his breath warm against her skin. "She's watching from the kitchen window, isn't she?"

Holly nodded, her hands resting on David's narrow waist.

"Holly, we're supposed to be engaged," he teased. "You don't want her to think you don't like me, do you."

Laughing softly, Holly reached up to kiss the corner of his mouth. "This is insane, David. It's Michael we're trying to convince. Do you really think Mom will approve of us necking in the backyard?"

"Humor me," he said softly. "She can tell Michael she caught us necking. Besides, she'd approve of this location more than a few other places I could think of." His lips played teasingly over hers. "I don't know what's more hazardous to my sanity, kissing you or not kissing you."

"Do you think we're shocking her?"

"She didn't get all these kids from a mail-order catalog," he stated with a low chuckle. He lifted his head to stare down at her. "Did she?"

Holly gave him a playful poke in the ribs. "I don't know! I was a Christmas present!"

David laughed. "No wonder you're such a nut. You got cheated out of all those birthday presents." Taking her hand in his, David moved toward the house.

"I never felt cheated," she said with a grin. "I was eight or nine years old before I would admit it wasn't *my* birthday the whole world was celebrating."

LATE THAT AFTERNOON Holly sat on a blanket on a grassy hillside in the park, watching David in what had started out as an action-packed, highly competitive game of touch football. It had changed quickly to an even tougher contest of tackle football. She shook her head in wonder, listening with a crooked grin to their grunts, groans and good-natured insults. One would think they were in a play-off game for the Super Bowl the way they took the game so seriously.

As she watched David, she wondered why she had ever worried about him fitting in with her family. Ron and Joe treated him as if he'd been around for years. Even Michael found some common ground with him. Holly had noticed the two deep in conversation for nearly an hour that morning. It had made her very nervous.

Then there were the children. For a while this afternoon, Holly thought David was the Pied Piper. To Bobby and Kevin he was the greatest thing since peanut butter and jelly, while Amy had him wrapped around her little finger in five minutes flat. If a man could be judged by his interaction with children, David would rank right up there with the best of them.

Holly's thoughts turned to the many facets of David Winslow. There was the serious side of him, the one she had seen first. That one was still a bit of a mystery to her. Then there was the fun side. She could still hear his whoop of joy upon beating her at Pac-Man. There was the competitive David, who would give all he had to a game of football. There was the side of him that knelt by a child and led that child through all the intricacies of building a boat that could successfully navigate the lone puddle of water down by the river.

Finally, there was the lusty, passionate David Winslow whom she couldn't think about without breaking out in a sweat.

Leaning back to rest on her elbows, Holly closed her eyes and raised her face to the sun. Weatherwise the day had been perfect. Soon it would be time to gather everything and everyone together and go back to the house. Far too soon it would be time to go home to Indianapolis.

Something hit the ground next to her with a solid thump. Her eyes popped open and it was all she could do to keep from laughing. David was sprawled face-down next to her on the blanket.

"Don't you dare laugh," he warned in a muffled voice. "I may die right here."

"And spoil the party tonight? You wouldn't dare!"

He opened one eye to glare up at her. "You are a cold hearted wench, Holly Nichols!" He let out a long, low groan. "Why did I let myself get talked into football! I'm far too old for this! It was safer building boats with the kids."

He let out another low moan and closed his eyes again. Holly took advantage of the opportunity to feast her eyes on his lean body, noting the way his damp T-shirt clung to the smooth muscles across his back and shoulders. Even being hot and sweaty didn't detract from his masculine appeal. Her hands itched to touch him, to feel those muscled arms holding her against him, to feel his work-roughened hands on her skin.

Her gaze moved down to his narrow waist, then further to where his Levi's stretched snugly across his taut derriere and muscular thighs. Damn, but he has nice buns, she thought wickedly.

Suddenly she was sprawled on the ground next to him, his strong fingers wrapped around her wrist, his eyes blazing. He was so close she could feel the warmth of his breath on her cheek.

"Do you like what you see?" he asked in a low, slightly ragged voice.

Holly licked her suddenly dry lips. The fire in his eyes burned to her very soul. "Yes," she managed to say with surprising bluntness, "I like it very much."

David drew in his breath with a soft hiss. "You're playing with fire, Holly." His eyes dropped to the thrust of her breasts against the stretchy fabric of her shirt, then shifted upward to the wildly beating pulse at the base of her throat. Moving his head only slightly, he pressed a soft kiss to that throbbing flesh.

Holly's skin tingled at his touch. How was it that this man could so quickly turn her mind to mush?

In a single lithe motion, David rolled away from her and stood, then reached down and pulled her to her feet.

"Walk down to the Plunge with me," he said, his eyes still blazing with sensuous heat. Holly had told him earlier about how the Plunge, a reservoir on the other side of the park, used to be a favorite necking spot for teenagers.

"We . . . we should be getting back."

"Holly, please." His eyes were filled with a deep longing. "I need to have you to myself, if just for a few minutes."

She couldn't resist his urgent plea. She didn't even try. Without a word she put her hand in his, and together they walked down the hill.

As soon as they were out of everyone's view, David pulled her into his arms for a long kiss that left them both breathless. She was trembling when he finally released her, and he was none too steady himself.

"There," he stated softly. "That should hold me for at least an hour." Looking down at the ripe fullness of her mouth, he chuckled. "Well, maybe a half hour...oh, hell!" He kissed her again, thoroughly.

Hand in hand they strolled along the edge of the reservoir. A hawk soared over head, the sun glistening off widespread wings. Holly watched until it disappeared from sight. It was quiet here. It felt good to be away from the noise and good-natured confusion that always marked a family gathering. She hadn't realized how badly she needed to be alone with David until now. That unnerved her.

"Your family is wonderful, Holly," David said, releasing her hand and draping his arm across her shoulders.

She put her arm around his waist. "Thanks. They think you're pretty wonderful, too."

They halted to look out over the smooth surface of the water, golden now in the rays of the lowering sun. David turned her into his arms and held her close. Would now be the time to broach the truth? He wanted to tell her the truth. Still he hesitated. He needed time to structure what he would say to her. A time when he wasn't so distracted by the warmth of her slender body pressed so comfortably against his.

Holly felt the soft brush of his lips against her cheek. Closing her eyes she gave herself up to the sheer perfection of the moment. If only it could be this way forever. She felt comfortable in his arms. At home.

Turning her head just a little, Holly found his lips with hers. Placing her hands on either side of his head, she kissed him tenderly, thoroughly, wanting to communicate to him how good she felt just being with him.

He held her as if she were a fragile piece of porcelain. His kiss was all the more tender for the fierce passion he held in control, all the more sensuous for its sweet tenderness.

Finally he eased away from her, resting his hands on her slim waist. "If we don't leave now, we won't leave at all." His voice was sandpapery rough, his eyes glowing with barely suppressed passion.

"Yes," she replied softly. "I think you're right. Someone will be sending out a search party shortly."

"Later," he promised against her lips before taking them in a last, searing kiss.

6

HOLLY STEPPED BACK from the three-tiered cake with a smile of satisfaction. The elegant confection, decorated in white and silver with a spray of tiny white roses on the top, was stunning. A silver-framed picture of Sam and Ellen taken on their wedding day rested between the two top tiers, providing the perfect finishing touch.

She heard the sound of cars pulling into the driveway, and within seconds the house was swarming with people, all exclaiming over the service, the cake, the gaily decorated house. Holly beamed proudly at her trim, attractive mother and big, handsome father.

Taking both of Ellen's hands in hers, she leaned forward to kiss her mom on the cheek. "Have I told you how lovely you look tonight, Mom?" The deep rose-colored dress Ellen wore suited her perfectly, and her smooth cheeks were flushed to a matching hue. At forty-seven she was still a stunning woman.

"I'd say both mother and daughter look downright beautiful tonight." David came up between them and slipped an arm around each woman's waist.

Sam scowled fiercely. "Not satisfied with stealing my daughter, young man? You have to capture her mother's heart, too?"

Ellen flushed a deeper shade of red. "You can't fault his taste, Sam," she teased lovingly.

Holly moved closer to David, reveling in the warmth of his body and the firm arm around her waist. Earlier she had been surprised and pleased when he came downstairs dressed in charcoal slacks, a burgundy blazer with a white shirt and a gray-and-burgundy striped tie. She hadn't even thought to mention clothes. It had been pure coincidence that his blazer matched her long gown.

"If you two would get a move on, we could celebrate your silver and our golden anniversary together," Sam growled. "Then we'd only have to survive one more of these get-togethers." The contented, happy light in his clear blue eyes completely belied his gruff words.

David's fingers tightened around Holly's waist. "Well, Sam, we're still working out some of the finer details. We seem to be having a little problem fitting it in between the Indy 500 and Frontier Days." He smiled lazily, ignoring Holly's soft gasp.

"Harrumph," Sam snorted. "The way you've been eyeballing Holly, you'd better do something damn quick!"

"Sam!" "Dad!" Ellen and Holly exclaimed in unison.

It didn't faze Sam one bit. His eyes danced with humor. "I understand your problem, son. It was the same way with me and her mother. Couldn't keep my hands off her. Finally had to hog-tie her and drag her to the altar."

Ellen gasped, her brown eyes flashing sparks while Holly couldn't decide whether to laugh or cry.

David was having a problem keeping a straight face, too. "Maybe you could give me a few pointers on handling these Nichols women."

"Sure thing, David," Sam said with a grin. "I'll have to tell you about the time Mama and I drove down to the Plunge and—"

"Sam Nichols, don't you dare!" Ellen's face was nearly the color of Holly's dress.

"What's going on here?" Michael stepped up and put one hand on Sam's shoulder and the other on Holly's. Deep blue eyes shone in his tanned, boyish face. He observed with interest the flaming faces of his mother and sister. "From the looks of things I arrived just in time."

Sam tilted his head toward David and Holly. "If you want to do something just in time, marry these two."

"Isn't one a night enough?" Michael asked, tossing David a conspiratorial wink. "Here I thought it was time to party and you're trying to put me to work again!" He nudged Sam. "You two are wanted over by the cake. About a dozen people are waiting to take your picture."

Sam groaned. "Come on, Mama, and let's get this over with. Maybe we'll take a drive down to the Plunge later just for old times' sake."

As they walked away, Ellen was glaring at Sam. "You might sleep in the barn tonight, too, Sam Nichols, just for old times' sake!"

"Michael!" Joe called for his brother, motioning him to the table where the cake sat. "Come on, Michael, we want you in the picture, too."

Left alone, David hugged Holly to him. "Do you get the feeling they're ganging up on us?" he whispered in her ear.

"You're not much help, David Winslow," she growled, feeling her insides melt when his breath danced across her skin. The entire day had been a challenge to her self-control.

"Wanna follow Sam and Ellen down to the Plunge later?"

Holly gazed deep into his eyes, captured as always by their clear green brilliance. "Whatever for?" she asked, her voice dripping with false innocence.

"Take a couple of guesses."

Holly couldn't suppress a smile. David was affecting the very same expression her two nephews used when they wanted something. His rough features softened, taking on a youthfulness that had been sorely lacking a couple of days ago.

"Why are you looking at me like that?"

Because I love you! Holly inhaled swiftly, sharply. She had almost spoken the words aloud. David's eyes narrowed, his sooty lashes almost meeting. Was it written all over her face? Or had she spoken without realizing it? "I—I was thinking about how different you look."

"Different?"

She nodded. "You look—younger, I think."

His hand cupped her chin, his roughened fingers warming the skin where he touched her. "Holly, I feel younger than I've felt in years. You've done that. You're like a ray of sunshine, a part of my life I didn't even know was missing. These past couple of days have been very special to me, and I'm not sure I want to see them end."

Holly was horrified to feel hot tears burning her eyes. The murmur of voices coming from the other side of the room, interspersed with laughter, played at the edge of her consciousness, but for all intents and purposes, David Winslow was the only other person in the world. How she wished things were different. How she wished she could tell him of her love for him, but she couldn't. Love meant pain, disillusionment, heartache, and she couldn't go through that again.

"David . . ."

"Hey, you lovebirds over there!" Sam's voice rang across the room. "You'd think you two were the only people here."

"Damn!" David swore softly. "We need to talk, Holly. There are so many things—"

David was interrupted by a chorus of voices, all wanting his attention. He looked at Holly with eyes shadowed by things she didn't understand, then walked away to join Joe and Rob.

Holly pondered David's words several hours later when things had quieted down. The pictures had all been taken, the cake had been cut and devoured with what seemed like gallons of homemade ice cream. Moms and dads were beginning to drift back after putting the little ones to bed. Everyone, as usual, gathered in the living room in clusters of three or four.

Holly sat alone in the corner of the couch, her feet curled beneath her. Someone put a record on the stereo and she knew the dancing would begin shortly. She didn't feel like dancing. All she wanted was to be alone, but she knew she couldn't for some time.

Feeling a tingling along the back of her neck, she looked up to sweep the room with her eyes. It was David, as she knew it would be. He stood near the fireplace with Sam and Ellen, his piercing gaze meeting and holding hers with the force of a magnet. He silently questioned her, the confusion at her sudden withdrawal mirrored in his expressive eyes. She broke the eye contact, dropping her gaze to her hands twisted in her lap. David was so intensely masculine, easy to be with, difficult to ignore and impossible to forget. How was she ever to manage it?

"Did you and David have an argument?"

Recognizing the familiar voice, Holly lifted her head to give her brother a weak smile. "Not exactly, Michael." Despite the role Michael had unwittingly played in her present predicament, Holly felt a surge of affection for this young man whom she'd never dreamed would become a minister. Talk about the terror of Valentine! With his sun-streaked blond hair and dark blue eyes, he looked more like a California beach boy than a man of the cloth, and those cobalt eyes of his still held a hint of the very devil himself.

"Having second thoughts about David, Sis?"

Second thoughts? *My dear brother,* she thought *I haven't even worked my way through the first batch yet.* Holly shrugged slightly. "I don't know, Michael. It's something I'm going to have to work out." Now would be a good time to tell him the truth. For weeks she had pictured the expression on his face when she told him.

Michael reached over to take her hand in his. "David is quite a guy, Holly. The whole family is impressed. He's so different from Rick." At the startled look of pain in her eyes, Michael flinched. "Does it still hurt after all this time? You're not still in love with Rick, are you?"

Her head snapped up in surprise. "Good heavens, no! But that whole experience has made me leery."

"Nobody could blame you for that," Michael said gently. "Holly, you've never said what happened to finally end your marriage, but I know you were deeply hurt by it. Don't let what happened in the past affect your relationship with David. Anyone can tell just by watching the two of you that he's crazy about you."

Holly cringed inwardly. This was not supposed to happen, she thought miserably. Michael shouldn't be sitting here being the understanding brother when she had attempted to play a joke on him. She shouldn't be sitting here wondering how to keep David in her life, a man she had advertised for in the newspaper! Things like this didn't happen in real life. Maybe she would wake up and it would all be a dream.

Knowing she couldn't let Michael know what was really bothering her, and admitting to herself that this was definitely not the time to tell him the truth, she managed a teasing grin. "Are you speaking from experience, Rev?"

Michael returned her grin with an impudence that didn't quite fit his somber apparel. "Why do I get the feeling you're not taking me seriously?"

Eyeing his black suit and white clerical collar, Holly chuckled. "Really, Michael! How can I take you seri-

ously when I can still see you and Heather Anderson at
the swimming—"

Michael clamped a hand over her mouth. "Holly
Carol Nichols, if you breathe a word of that I'll tell
about the time you put a certain chocolate-flavored
'medicine' in the frosting on Willie Jenson's birthday
cake!"

Holly's eyes widened and she threw her hands up in
surrender. Michael removed his hand from her mouth
and they both burst into laughter. When they were able
to speak again, Holly leaned over to kiss Michael on the
cheek.

"You know I'm very proud of you, Michael James
Nichols," she said softly.

"Just keep on being my friend, Holly."

Her eyes darkened dangerously. "I will, as long as
you don't announce my engagement from the pulpit—
especially when I'm not engaged at the time."

To her surprise, two bright spots of red appeared on
Michael's tanned cheeks. "I'm really sorry about that,
Holly," he said.

"You are?"

"Yes," Michael admitted. "If I had known about David I wouldn't have done that, but you never mentioned him." He smiled his crooked smile. "I just want
you to be happy, and to be my friend."

Holly was too shocked to delve deeper into the phe-
nomenon of Michael's apology. Besides, how could she
give him a difficult time about it when the evidence of
her own deception stood not fifteen feet from them?
"Oh, hell, Michael," she said irreverently. "We have to

be friends. We know too much about each other to ever be enemies."

Just then Sam's voice boomed across the room. "Let's get this party going! I thought we were going to dance!"

"Guess it's time for me to make my exit," Michael said in a low voice.

"Whatever for?" Holly exclaimed. "You can't leave now, the party's just starting."

"I know." He winked, loosening his collar. "That's why I'm going upstairs to change into something more appropriate. Besides, you don't need me to keep you company. Here comes David."

Before she could make a move to escape, Holly was lifted off the couch and swung into David's arms.

"I've been waiting for this all evening," he growled, slipping his arms around her to pull her against him. Some romantic soul had turned off almost all the lamps in the room, creating a seductive atmosphere.

Holly's pulse leaped when David whirled her around, his lean body moving with smooth, athletic grace. "For someone who's been stuck in a monastery, you certainly dance well," she murmured.

"That's the nicest thing you've said to me in a couple of hours, Ms. Nichols."

"Oh, don't let it go to your head, Mr. Winslow. I was thinking of my poor bare feet." Lord, he smelled good! Whatever brand of after-shave he wore should be outlawed. The stuff was downright lethal.

His arm tightened, pulling her closer to the warmth of his body. "And here I thought it was because you were looking for a chance to get close to me."

Jackets and ties had long since been discarded and Holly could feel the heat of him through the thin fabric of his shirt.

"Why have you been avoiding me, Holly?"

David's husky voice in her ear sent tremors of pleasure through her. What in the world was she going to say? That her plan had backfired and she'd fallen in love with him?

"Holly..." he began warningly. Then he stopped, laughter rumbling deep in his chest as his arms slid from around her. "Good grief, even the minister in this family is wacko!"

Holly stared up at him in confusion, then turned around to see what David was talking about. Michael stood at the foot of the stairs, his black coat and clerical collar replaced by a bright red T-shirt emblazoned with a white heart and the words Nebraska's Valentine.

She turned back to look up at David, a challenge in her eyes. "Something wrong with that?" she asked.

Shaking his head, David studied her upturned face. "Do you have a T-shirt like that?"

Without thinking, she answered, "Of course! I wear it for a nightgown."

David's eyes glittered, his arms drawing her to him once again. Bending his head, he brushed his mouth along the sensitive skin below her ear. "Will you wear it for me sometime?"

A shudder racked Holly's body at the image that suggestion conjured up. She felt so weak her fingers dug into the solid muscles of David's back for support. For the life of her, she couldn't force one coherent word past her lips.

David's low, husky voice continued. "Wear it for me, Holly, so I can take it off you and kiss every single inch of your soft skin that it hid from me."

"David . . ." she murmured, closing her eyes only to see an image of herself naked, with David trailing warm kisses across her bare skin.

"And then I'm going to make love to you until neither of us can walk," he whispered raspingly. His hand traced a slow pattern of fire up and down her spine, nudging her closer, molding her to him. "I want you, Holly, more than I've ever wanted any woman in my life."

Holly opened her eyes to look dazedly around the room. Did her family know she was being seduced right in the middle of the living room? Daring to look up at him, she whispered, "David, have you forgotten where we are?"

"No, I haven't forgotten," he said, the huskiness lingering in his low voice. "It's the only reason I have any control at all."

"You call this control?" She was blatantly aware of how far his seduction had gone. Every nerve in her body tingled. Her breasts, pressed against his chest, were taut with desire, and her legs were totally useless for anything remotely resembling the function they were designed for.

"You want me, too, Holly," he went on relentlessly, mesmerized by the golden lights in her warm brown eyes. She was soft and warm and so damn desirable she took his breath away.

"Would you two be interested in the fact that the music stopped at least five minutes ago?"

Startled, Holly jumped away from the warmth of David's embrace. Suddenly everyone in the room applauded and Sam was grinning at them like a Cheshire cat.

"Believed me, didn't you!" His blue eyes sparkled with devilry as he glared teasingly at David. "I'd like to dance with my daughter, Winslow. That is, if you can tear yourself away from her long enough. Don't much fancy dancing with both of you."

David gave him a mock bow. "Be my guest, Sam. Maybe I'll just round up that pretty wife of yours for this dance."

"That boy's treading on thin ice," Sam growled, gazing down at Holly's flushed face with tender affection. "I see he's got you all hot and bothered again."

"Dad!" she exclaimed, her cheeks flushing. "You're impossible!"

Sam hugged her. "I know. You mama tells me that all the time."

A swift rush of love for this man washed over her. Sam Nichols was the best father a girl could ask for. "This has been quite a day, hasn't it? How does it feel to be married for twenty-five years?"

"Truth?" Sam was serious, his blue eyes wistful. "I don't know where the years have gone. Seems like only yesterday you were just a little mite, hell-bent on driving me into an early grave. Now look at you! All grown-up, independent as hell, a successful businesswoman and pretty as a picture."

"Think of all the peace and quiet you have now," Holly reminded him, unsettled by Sam's words.

"It's almost too quiet, Holly Carol. But the years have been good years." His voice took on an added gruffness. "You know, by the time your mama was your age, she had seven kids."

"Now, Dad," Holly protested, "you're not going to start on me, are you?"

"Nope!" he stated in a low voice. "I've never interfered in your life and I don't intend to start now. But I want you to know your mother and I like David a lot. We're sorry this engagement thing is a hoax." He eyed Holly closely. "It is a hoax, isn't it?"

Holly nodded, fighting to hide her turmoil. She had to admit that, like Sam and Ellen, she too was beginning to wish it was no hoax.

The music stopped, but Holly stood there with Sam's arms around her, wondering if the joke would turn out to be on her. Putting her arms around her father's neck, she hugged him fiercely. "I love you, Dad," she said. "You know that, don't you?"

"Reckon I do, Holly Carol," he said in a voice rough with emotion. "All your mother and I want is for you to be happy."

"You don't have to worry about Holly's happiness, Sam. I intend to take very good care of her."

At the sound of David's voice, Holly dropped her gaze to the floor and Sam chuckled. "You'd better do something with this girl damn quick, son. Things are getting out of hand." He patted David on the shoulder and walked away.

Shaken by the depth of her emotions, Holly averted her face from David. "I think I'll get some fresh air."

She whirled and fled into the kitchen, then out the back door, not bothering to stop for a sweater or to remember her shoes. In stocking feet, she ran across the backyard and down into the woods, following the path to her spot by the creek. The night air was chilly and damp, but she didn't notice. Miserable to the core of her being, she ran to the huge elm tree and leaned her forehead against it, letting the tears flow. She sobbed quietly, digging her fingers into the rough bark, longing to scream out her frustration and misery. How could she have been so incredibly stupid?

Suddenly, instead of the cold tree, she found herself cradled against the warmth and strength of a human body. David's low voice whispered in her ear, "It takes a nutso, dippy lady to run into the night air without shoes or a sweater." Holding her shuddering body close, he caressed her gently. "What is it, Holly? What happened?"

Knowing she was overreacting, but still unable to speak, Holly just shook her head and burrowed against David's warmth. He held her for a long time, caressing her until her sobbing stopped and she stood quietly in his arms.

"Oh, David," she said at last. "I've really made a mess of things and I don't know how to fix any of it."

"What do you mean?" Setting her away from him, he gazed down at her troubled features. "Did you tell Michael the truth? I saw you talking to him a while ago."

Holly shook her head. "No, I didn't. I couldn't." She clenched her fists in frustration. "I don't know what went wrong! What started out as a practical joke has snowballed into something out of control!"

"Sometimes a practical joke has a way of doing that," David said softly. "But, Holly, you never meant to hurt anyone by this."

"Somehow that isn't much comfort right now," she said miserably. "Everyone is hoping our 'engagement' will become a reality. Even Dad told me how wonderful he and Mom think you are."

"Well," David said with a low laugh, "you can't fault their taste."

"David!" Holly stepped away and began pacing back and forth. "I didn't plan on this," she said.

David moved to stand in front of her, his hands coming up to take her shoulders in a warm grip. "There are a lot of things about this weekend that neither of us planned on, Holly," he said in an odd but gentle tone. "It all started as a lark and has turned into something much more serious. When I walked into your office the other night, I had no idea I'd meet a brown-eyed imp who would turn my life upside down. I didn't plan on meeting two people as special as Sam and Ellen." He released her shoulders to cup her face with his warm hands. "We can work it out, Holly. Neither of us counted on this turning out the way it has. Least of all me. Do you have any idea what this weekend has meant to me, Holly? I lost my parents when I was fifteen years old. Sure, I've got brothers and sisters, but I was too busy trying to hold us all together to gain any closeness with them until the past few years. Seeing you with your family has meant a lot to me."

He slipped his arms around her waist and pulled her against him. "Damn it, Holly, this isn't the time to go into all that. It wasn't very smart of you to run that ad. We would have met eventually, in a more orthodox manner, but it wouldn't have been nearly as much fun." Bending his head, he touched his lips to hers. "You didn't really think I was going to let you go after this weekend, did you?"

"I was hoping you wouldn't," she whispered, moving closer to feel his mouth settle more fully over hers. There were so many questions she wanted to ask about his family and the things he had just revealed, but they would have to wait. Right now there were more pressing issues to deal with. "You're not what I expected at all, David Winslow. You scare the hell out of me."

"That makes two of us," he admitted, "because the way I feel about you has *me* scared half to death."

"Oh, David," she moaned, leaning into his rock-hard strength. "What are we going to do?"

He stared down at her for a long, pulsing moment; her features were barely visible in the darkness, but he didn't need light to see her. Everything about her was imbedded in his mind from her mass of honey-brown curls and her impish sherry-colored eyes fringed with gold-tipped lashes to the lush fullness of her mouth and the spattering of freckles across her pert nose. The musical sound of her laughter invaded his dreams at night. The memory of her silken skin, of her small breasts fitting his hands so perfectly, had the power to keep him awake for hours.

"Ahh, Holly," he groaned, surrendering to the temptation of her lips hovering so close to his. He took her mouth possessively, hungrily, his tongue meeting hers in a hot duel for supremacy. Lean fingers dug into her spine, curving her slender body against his as he feasted ever more deeply on the sweetness she so willingly offered.

Holly clung to him, absorbing his warmth, drawn swiftly into a passion that threatened to consume her. Nothing mattered beyond this moment, holding David and being held by him. Her hands roamed over him, aching for the feel of his smooth skin under her fingertips. Waves of pleasure rolled through her as his hands slid up her rib cage to cup her breasts.

"Holly," he whispered, her name a soft cadence as his lips roved relentlessly over her face and neck. Lowering her slowly to the grassy earth beneath them, he sought her lips in a tender, passionate kiss that left her weak and trembling.

Taking her hand, he spread it flat against his chest. "Touch me, Holly," he commanded in a low voice that was rough with passion. Parting the tiny buttons at the bodice of her dress, he swept the soft fabric aside to bare her breasts to the chill night air. "I need to have you touch me."

Holly began fumbling with the buttons of his shirt, a low moan of pleasure escaping her as she came in contact with the crisply curling hair on his muscular chest. She ran her hands greedily up and down his rib cage, reveling in the feel of him beneath her fingertips. His skin was like smooth satin stretched over steel.

The touch of his hand on her breast was light and almost painfully teasing. The tip hardened immediately, begging for more of his touch. She inhaled sharply when his lips brushed the sensitive skin. He nipped gently with his teeth, then drew her nipple fully into his mouth with an erotic motion that sent Holly's body arching against him.

Slipping his arms around her, David cushioned her from the hard ground as he teased and tantalized each breast in turn before moving his mouth back to hers. He locked his arms around her, then rolled over on his back, bringing her to lie on top of him. Emboldened by the pleasure he had given her, Holly began a sensuous exploration of her own.

Her lips trailed along the smooth line of his jaw, down the corded column of his neck, grazed over his collarbone and came to rest at the wildly beating pulse at the base of his throat.

"Holly!" His breath was ragged and uneven. "Do you know what you do to me?" His hands cupped either side of her head, his fingers splayed through her hair.

"The same thing you're doing to me," she answered raggedly. She was sprawled full-length atop him, fiercely aware of his arousal even through the layers of their clothing. Holly was entranced by her power over him. Her searching fingers found the flat male nipple nestled in the thick mat of hair and teased it to button hardness.

David's swift intake of breath signaled his pleasure. His fingers dug into her scalp, bringing her mouth back to his. Slowly his lips softened, his fingers loosened to trail along the curve of her neck, the fiery passion of his caresses easing to a tender, feather-light touch.

"Holly," he murmured against her lips. "If we don't stop now we'll be past the point of no return, and I don't want our first time to be on a creek bank." David took a long shaky breath and exhaled slowly. "Though heaven knows, I want you so much I ache with it."

Laying her head on his chest, Holly listened to the strong rapid beat of his heart, too overcome by all the new sensations raging inside her to speak. Thank goodness David still had enough control to call a halt before they'd gone any further.

"Do you think Sam will come looking for me with a shotgun pretty soon?"

Lifting her head, Holly kissed the cleft of his chin. "Probably." She chuckled softly. "Besides, how will it look if we both came down with a virulent case of pneumonia?"

"Damn sight better than lead poisoning," he muttered.

Holly's hand came up to caress his cheek. "David," she whispered, "I've never felt like this before. Not with anyone."

He turned his head, kissing the palm of her hand. "Nor have I."

Neither spoke for a long moment, then Holly rose awkwardly and began putting her clothing in order. She watched David button his shirt and tuck it into the waistband of his slacks, then looked up to meet his gaze in the darkness.

David brushed her hair back from her face, his knuckles grazing her skin. The mere touch of his hand sent a tremor of desire and need coursing through her. "You look a mess, Ms. Nichols," he teased her, "just like you've been rolling in the hay."

Holly stared at him for a moment, then burst into laughter. "You don't look so hot yourself, city boy. Your hair is all mussed and I'll bet you have grass stains all over the back of your shirt."

Wrapping her arms around his neck, Holly smoothed his hair as best she could. "Maybe we can sneak in and nobody will see us."

He dropped a light kiss on the tip of her nose. "We can always go through the kitchen and sneak up the back stairs."

Holly's eyes darkened with suspicion. The back stairs were rarely used, being closed off, dark and narrow. "How do you know about the back stairs?"

"Michael told me," he said, picking several blades of grass from her hair. "He told me he used to sneak down the back stairs when he wanted to slip out and meet some girl named Heather Anderson."

Holly's eyes narrowed. "What else did that brother of mine tell you?"

David grasped her wrists from around his neck. Slipping an arm around her waist, he drew her snugly against his side and began to move in the direction of the house. "I promised I wouldn't tell," he stated in a tone of pious innocence. The laughter in his voice gave him away.

"I'll strangle him with my bare hands," she threatened fiercely. "Just wait till I see him. Minister or not, I'll get him."

"You can't do bodily harm to Nebraska's Valentine, Holly," he said, turning her into his arms for a quick kiss. "Besides, I learned a lot."

No one had ever made her lose her train of thought as quickly as this man. She could barely remember what they'd been talking about now that she was pressed against his lean body and his lips were so enticingly close. "What did you learn?"

"I learned you've always been nutso and dippy. That it wasn't something you acquired with age."

"Then kiss this nutso, dippy person and let's get in the house before they send a search party after us."

David complied willingly, taking her mouth in a long, drugging kiss. "The house is dark," he said, nibbling her lower lips. "Do you think it's safe for us to go in?"

"Let's be daring," Holly retorted, her tears of an hour ago forgotten.

7

DAVID HELD the back door open and waited until Holly entered the kitchen, then stepped inside and pulled the door shut behind him. As quietly as possible, they made their way across the room.

Holly stopped so suddenly that David bumped into her. Biting her lip to keep from laughing, she turned to David and pointed across the dimly lit room. There, in the circle of light cast by the small bulb over the stove, oblivious to the presence of anyone but each other, stood Sam and Ellen, locked in a passionate embrace.

Smiling, David motioned for Holly to move on. She took a step and promptly crashed into a chair, the clatter reverberating throughout the kitchen.

"What in tarnation!" Still holding Ellen firmly in his arms, Sam looked up, pinning David and Holly with a baleful glare. "Oh, hell, I should have know! Darn kids are all grown and they're still interrupting at the damnedest times!"

"Uh, we're sorry, sir," David apologized, his lips twitching. "We didn't think anyone was still up."

"Think nothing of it, son," Sam grumbled. "You get used to it after all these years. Why do you think it took five years for us to get those twins?" Releasing a smiling Ellen, he went on. "Between one kid needing a drink of water, another seeing monsters in the closet and the rest taking ten trips to the bathroom, we had to sneak away to the barn to have any privacy."

"Oh, Sam, it wasn't that bad," Ellen protested affectionately. "Would you two like to join us for a cup of coffee? That's what we came in here for."

"Is that what it's called?" David teased.

"You've got a lot of room to talk," Sam stated, his piercing blue eyes raking the younger couple. "You two been down to the creek?"

Holly flushed hotly, aware of her and David's rumpled state. "I needed some fresh air."

"From the looks of you, you got more than fresh air." Sam's eyes twinkled as he crossed the room and settled his big frame onto one of the oak chairs at the huge table. He motioned for Holly and David to do the same. "Did you two get married while you were out?"

"Oh, Sam, stop!" Ellen scolded, taking four mugs from the cabinet and filling them with fresh-brewed coffee. "Why don't you leave these poor children alone?"

David turned to Holly and winked.

Ellen set the mugs of coffee on the table and sat down next to Sam. "I hate to see you two leave tomorrow. Can't you stay another day or two?"

Holly shook her head in regret. "I have to get back to work, Mom. After all, I am the boss."

"And I have appointments scheduled for Monday that I can't change," David said, reaching for Holly's hand under the table.

Lacing her fingers through his, Holly picked up her cup with the other hand and took a drink of the steaming brew. David's thumb rubbed sensuous circles on the back of her hand and it was all she could do to concentrate on the conversation. "I have an appointment Monday I wouldn't mind missing," Holly muttered, thinking of the scheduled meeting with D. W. Branson. Unless he canceled that, too, she thought in resentment.

"That's part of being the boss, Holly Carol," Sam said. "It comes with the territory."

Holly nodded. "I know, but I sure wish there was a way out of this one. You knew the building where my office is located was sold some time ago to a hot-shot investor. Well, he's decided to tear it down and he wants to meet with all the tenants on Monday to explain why."

David tensed, arranging his features into the expressionless mask that had served him so well through ten years of boardroom skirmishes.

"Holly, I'm sorry!" Ellen exclaimed. "When did you find out about all of this?"

Holly shrugged, not wanting to spoil a wonderful evening by bringing up the subject of D. W. Branson. Already she felt her anger surfacing again. It had been easy to forget all this during the past few days. "We got a notice from Branson himself just last week that he wanted to arrange a meeting with all of us," she stated, "but we had already heard through the grapevine that he was going to destroy the building."

"Didn't you tell us a couple of months ago that he was going to do extensive renovations?" Sam asked. "What happened to that idea?"

"The renovations were started, and from the looks of it he was going to do a wonderful job," Holly explained with a frown. "Then, for some reason, he just stopped."

"Maybe he ran into some problems he didn't expect," David said in a low voice.

"David could be right, Holly," Ellen put in.

Holly's mouth tightened in annoyance. "Hah! That building has been there for years. D. W. Branson just decided to tear it down so he could put up one of those awful high rises. As if there aren't enough of them already!"

David fought the urge to tell her how much money he had already sunk into that building, and for what? It was his first foray into renovation and he had been looking forward to it with relish. He wanted to tell her of his own deep disappointment upon learning of the building's weaknesses, weaknesses that left him no choice but to raze it.

Sam's forehead wrinkled in a frown. "Sounds to me like you're taking this real personal, Holly. What have you got against D. W. Branson, anyway?"

"I've heard a lot about him," Holly said, her eyes bright with scorn. "He started from nothing a dozen or so years ago and now he's one of the biggest, richest, most powerful developers in Indianapolis, maybe in the entire state. A real self-made millionaire. I read where he's put several smaller contractors out of business over the years. There's no telling how many people he's destroyed on his way to the top."

David released her hand, standing abruptly to move to the counter, where he refilled his cup. He turned around to lean back against the counter, his face carefully void of all expression, save for the rythmic flexing of the muscle in his jaw. Pain lanced through him at the scorn in Holly's voice when she spoke D. W. Branson's name. The situation was far more serious than he had imagined. Through the years he had never cared what people thought of him, nor had he rebutted the slanted stories and lies written about him. Those who counted knew the truth. The rest didn't matter.

Damn! He had never thought it would mean so much to him. The incident that had turned him against all that public exposure had happened so long ago he had all but forgotten the details. Strangely enough, the story bore a striking similarity to what had happened between Holly and her brother. But in his case, people had ended up getting hurt—badly. He had been dating a woman for several months, Melanie Wakefield, the only daughter of a wealthy family. Old money. Old values. His and Melanie's picture had appeared in the society section of the paper every week as they attended this ball or that charity function. It got so they couldn't go out for a drive without it being mentioned in someone's column the next day.

David hated that feeling of living in a fishbowl, of having his private life spread all over the paper for the entire world to see. Besides, his relationship with Melanie was fast reaching a dead end. He had decided to break things off when their engagement was announced in the paper. Furious, David tracked down the culprit, a reporter who told him she had heard it from an unimpeachable source. He demanded she print a retraction, but the damage had been done.

The anger and pain of that incident had faded long ago, but his aversion to the press lingered until this day.

It was irrational, he knew, but there nonetheless. It didn't surprise him that Holly had never seen D. W. Branson's picture in the paper. He had wanted it that way.

"Holly, you should know better than to listen to gossip," her mother scolded.

"It can't all be just gossip, Mom. I've seen his name in the paper linked with at least a dozen women over the past few years. As for his business dealings, where there's smoke there must be fire. You know how I feel about men like him, men who have no scruples when it comes to women or business."

"That's a pretty harsh generalization, Holly," Sam interjected. "It isn't like you to judge a man without meeting him." David's gaze lifted to meet Sam's. He saw the suspicion in Sam's eyes. "You haven't met this D. W. Branson," Sam said quietly, "have you?"

"No," Holly admitted, scowling as she remembered Branson's cowardice. "He made an appointment to meet with me, then canceled it." She didn't see David's eyebrows arch in surprise or the sudden comprehension in his dark eyes.

"Why did he want to meet with just you?" Sam asked. "Didn't you say he was meeting with all the tenants on Monday?"

Holly shifted in her seat. "I wrote to him several times but didn't receive an answer." Her eyes flashed. "At least, not until I threatened him with a court injunction."

"Holly!"

She looked at her mother, her chin set at a stubborn angle. "He can't just tear that building down without a reason," she protested. "And I'll fight him every inch of the way."

Sam leaned back in his chair, his arms resting across his broad chest as he watched David through half-closed eyes. "Maybe this Branson fella has good reason to tear the building down, like David said." His gaze shifted back to Holly. "If he does, you're going to look mighty foolish trying to get an injunction."

Holly stared at her father. "Just whose side are you on, Dad? D. W. Branson deserves to be taken down a notch or two, and I just might be the person to do it! If nothing else, it will make him stop for once and think about what he's doing! He has to realize he can't walk over people all his life and get away with it!"

David paled, stricken by the venom in Holly's voice. He had not stopped to consider that her anger at D. W. Branson would run so deep. He watched Ellen move closer to Holly and soon, when mother and daughter were involved in a quiet, private conversation, he slipped out of the house to the back porch, breathing deeply of the cool, humid night air. Fog was beginning to hover over the creek, and long fingers of mist swirled around the thick trunks of trees and crept across the lawn. He reached in his pocket for a cigarette, then remembered he had quit the habit five years ago. He'd give his right arm for a cigarette right now.

Leaning a hip against the railing, he stared out into the darkness. Sam knew. David was certain of it. When he heard the opening and closing of the door behind him, he knew who it was without turning around. His body tensed in readiness for what was to come. There was a long drawn-out silence before Sam spoke. David wasn't prepared for the gentleness in Sam's gravelly voice.

"When are you going to tell her, son?"

There was no use pretending he didn't know what Sam was talking about.

"It wasn't supposed to turn out like this," he said quietly. He heard Sam settle himself into the rocker behind him and turned to face the older man. "I'm not sure where to begin."

"You don't owe me an explanation. I thought Holly's bringing you here for the weekend was part of a joke on Michael. Seems to me it's much more complicated than that."

"Complicated" was an understatement, David thought. "I love her, Sam."

"I suspected as much."

"But I've only known her for two days."

Sam looked at little surprised at that, then shrugged his broad shoulders. "I knew Ellen all my life, but I fell in love with her in one afternoon."

They talked for more than an hour, right up until Holly stepped out onto the porch looking for David. Sam stood to give Holly a light peck on the cheek and to say good-night, then turned to David and held out his hand.

"I've enjoyed our talk, David," he said. "I wish you all the best." He held David's gaze for a long moment before releasing his hand. "Just remember what I've told you."

After he went inside, Holly turned to David. "What was that all about?"

Instead of answering, David put his arms around her and drew her close, holding her as though he would never let her go. Time was running out. Time he needed to convince her that nothing in his life held any meaning without her.

Holly sensed the desperation in the strong arms holding her. Cupping the back of his head, she gazed deep into his troubled green eyes. "What is it, David?"

He bent his head and kissed her gently. "Would you believe that I was wishing we could take your mother up on her invitation to stay longer?" *Long enough for you to love me as I love you,* he added silently. *Long enough for you to be able to forgive me for the lies.*

Holly wrapped her arms around his waist and, leaning her head on his chest, listened to his strong steady heartbeat. "It would be nice, wouldn't it. It doesn't seem possible that our time here is almost over."

"Holly," he murmured thickly, "there's so little time." Wrapping his arms more tightly around her, he fitted his mouth to hers with a hunger he doubted would ever be completely sated.

THE LIGHTS of Omaha shone murkily through a fog so thick they could barely see. Flicking a glance at David, Holly sensed his tension. They had been driving through the dense fog for nearly one hundred miles, their progress slowed to a crawl.

Attempting a smile to hide her trepidation, she said flippantly, "Nice night for a murder."

David took his eyes off the highway to flash Holly a rueful glance. "Great thought, Holly. It might be perfect for a homicide but not for flying."

Holly looked out the window at the thick swirling mist. "You don't really think they'll close the airport, do you?"

"If it keeps getting worse, I don't see how they can avoid it. Nobody can see in this pea soup, let alone fly in it."

"Oh, David," Holly scoffed. "Those big airliners fly by instruments. Who needs to see?"

"Would you get in an airplane if you knew the pilot was flying blind?"

Holly lifted her shoulders in a shrug. "No, I was just trying to keep your mind off the fact that this fog is getting thicker by the minute. I can't even see past the hood."

David checked the clock on the dashboard. "Our flight time is only an hour away." The mist thinned long enough for him to make out the familiar red-and-white sign of a national motel chain looming out of the murky fog. "I think I'll stop and call the airport. There's no sense in driving that far if the flight has been canceled anyway."

A few minutes later he pulled the small car into the parking lot and found a vacant space. "I'll go make a few calls, Holly. Wait here and I'll be back as soon as I can."

"You won't lose me in this fog, will you?"

David leaned over and kissed her lightly on the corner of her mouth. "I've waited thirty-four years to find you. I'll be damned if I'm going to lose you now."

He got out of the car and Holly watched him move through the mist until he was nothing but an illusive shadow appearing and reappearing in the darkness.

What was she to do if the planes were grounded and she was forced to spend the night in Omaha, alone with David? The prospect was far more appealing than she was willing to admit.

Still, despite her attempts to exorcise them, the ghosts of her old insecurities lingered. The bottom line was that she was scared. Scared she wouldn't measure up. Scared she would disappoint David, even though her touch seemed to spark the same breathless response in him that his touch did in her.

Holly still hadn't solved all the puzzles or sorted out her confusion when David returned. She rolled down the window when he approached the car and smiled up at him.

David rested his forearm on the door and leaned down. "Hi, funny face. Did you miss me?"

How could one man be so downright disturbing? The damp mist had curled his hair into an even more unruly mass than usual. He smelled of rain and clean air, and his mouth hovered so close she had to fight the urge to move the few inches that would close the gap.

Her lips parted in a slow smile. "One of the things I love about you, city boy, is your unerring ability to choose such charming, flattering nicknames for *moi!*"

Reaching through the open window to touch his forefinger to the throbbing pulse at the base of her throat, he gazed at her through lowered lashes. "One of the things?" he whispered in a voice of velvet-edged steel. "You mean there are others?"

The blood leaped through her veins at his touch. David pressed his finger more firmly against her pulse, and it was suddenly difficult for her to breathe.

"I . . . I . . ." she stuttered, then gave up. Not only had he stolen her breath, he had stolen her capacity for speech. Struggling to control her body's reaction to his touch, Holly took a deep, shuddering breath. David withdrew his hand and she exhaled slowly. How would it look if she pulled him right through the window?

"Are you hungry?"

In more ways than one, Holly thought. "Starved," she said. "I take it we're stranded?"

"I'm afraid so," he said, looking anything but sorry. "The fog is expected to lift in a few hours, but the next flight to Indianapolis isn't scheduled until six in the morning. I was lucky enough to book the last available room and there's a nice restaurant where we can have dinner."

BY THE TIME they had eaten dinner and finally reached their room, a tight knot of tension clutched Holly's insides. David unlocked the door and nudged her into the room with a gentle hand on the small of her back.

"Not bad, as these places go," he said.

Holly didn't notice anything but the bed, which seemed to take on gigantic proportions in the spacious room. During the past hour butterflies had taken up residence in her stomach and were now holding a gymnastics competition there.

Tossing the keys on the dresser, David turned to her. "I'll bring the luggage in from the car while you freshen up." He grinned devilishly. "Should I take the key with me or will you let me back in?"

Turning startled eyes to him, Holly moistened her suddenly dry lips with the tip of her tongue. She knew she was acting like an adolescent schoolgirl, but she couldn't seem to retain her balance around him. Knowing she wouldn't be able to utter one coherent word, she simply nodded her head, wondering at David's low laugh when he pocketed the key and left.

After the door closed behind him, Holly searched the room with frantic eyes. It was a basic run-of-the-mill motel room, identical to thousands of others across the country. Besides the bed there was a dresser, a table with two chairs and a lamp, a television and a clock radio. She didn't have to check to know that the television and radio were bolted down, or open the dresser drawer to know it was well supplied with stationery, pens, postcards and the ubiquitous Gideon Bible.

Then why was she so nervous?

Maybe it was because, of all the places in the world she could be tonight, this was exactly where she *wanted* to be. She loved David, she finally admitted to herself. And he loved her. Holly was certain of it.

She went into the bathroom to freshen up as best she could until David came back with her suitcase. She was drying her face when she heard him return. Avoiding his direct gaze, Holly went to get the things she needed from her suitcase, then retreated back into the bathroom. Lingering far longer than necessary, she finally opened the door to find David leaning against the wall, smiling in amusement.

"I was beginning to think you'd fallen asleep in the bathtub."

"Sorry," she murmured, slipping past him.

The door closed behind him and within a few seconds Holly heard the shower. Trying to act as nonchalant as possible under the circumstances, she looked down at her clothes and wondered if she should sleep in them or change into something more . . . something else. She smoothed the crisp fabric of her cream-colored slacks, then fumbled with the ruffle at the neck of her jade blouse. The matching jacket lay tossed on the end of the bed next to David's windbreaker. How she wished she could be more blasé about spending the night with a man in a motel room.

Holly strolled to the window and parted the drapes, looking out at the thick swirling fog. For perhaps the hundredth time she wondered what to do about the situation she found herself in. She wanted David. There was no doubt in her mind about that. But what if he didn't want her? This seduction business was more complicated than she could ever have dreamed.

"Holly—"

The husky sound of her name sent frissons of awareness through her. She hadn't heard the shower stop or the bathroom door open, yet when she turned ever so slightly, David was right beside her. He was wearing nothing but the form-fitting Levi's he'd worn for the drive from Valentine. His bare chest gleamed with moisture, as did his raven hair. Muscles rippled beneath his bare flesh as he reached out to hand her something.

"What's this?" she asked, taking the folded paper from him.

"It's the contract."

She didn't understand why he was concerned about the contract now. Together they had managed to make mincemeat of it over the weekend. She looked up at him in confusion. Yet his reference to the contract reminded her of another part of their agreement. Stepping away from him for a moment, she reached into her purse and withdrew a long white envelope.

David frowned. "What . . . ?"

"It's the last of the money," she said quickly, hating to have to deal with this part of their arrangement.

David's eyes darkened for a moment, then he smiled. Slowly he tore up the envelope with the check inside and dropped the pieces into the trash can. "To hell with the money, Holly," he whispered raggedly, dragging her into his arms. "It isn't important now."

Holly swallowed convulsively, vitally aware of his warm male body pressing against her. "What is?"

His finger traced the line of her jaw. "That contract lacked a few very important provisions."

Her skin tingled where he touched her. In the dim light she could see the burning intensity of his eyes. "Like what?" she whispered, entranced by the lines feathering out from the corners of his eyes.

His voice was so low she had to move closer to hear him. She felt his warmth, caught the clean scent of soap and water, felt the dampness emanating from his bare skin. "It fails to mention what happens when the hired fiancé falls in love with the boss lady."

Holly's heart beat a rapid tattoo against her rib cage. Closing her eyes, she took a deep shaky breath. Was this just a ploy to get her into bed? Could she trust him? Oh, how she wanted to.

"Look at me, Holly," he commanded gruffly. When she opened her eyes, he saw a shimmering brightness. "I love you." The fingers that lightly touched the side of her neck trembled as he lowered his head to capture her mouth in a slow, tender kiss that robbed her of coherent thought. Gathering her into his arms, he held her tightly, whispering soft words in her ear. His lips trailed a burning path along the curve of her neck to the collar of her blouse.

"David," she murmured, burying her face against the moist warmth of his bare chest. "We've only known each other for three days. How can you be sure?"

She was soft and warm. Woman soft—woman warm. "Because when you've been looking for something all your life, it makes it easier to recognize when you finally find it. I think I fell in love with you the moment you ordered me into your office and started rattling off all those restrictions on how I was to behave this weekend."

"I think I fell in love with you over the Orange Julius in the mall, when I thought you were going to kiss me in front of all those people."

"I was tempted. Were you terribly disappointed?"

She tilted her head back to look up at him. "Terribly, but if you start making up for it now, I'll consider forgiving you for that one little slip."

"Holly, I'm not looking for a one-night stand with you," he declared softly. "I love you, more than I thought it possible to love another human being. If you think I'm going to let you walk out of my life, you're wrong." His eyes darkened. How was he to explain to her that she belonged in his life and in his bed? He had never felt so possessive toward anyone in his life.

Quivering from the touch of his fingers against her skin, Holly met his smoldering gaze. "I want you so much, David," she whispered.

"Trust me, Holly." He saw the desire in her eyes, recognized the want and the need. With fingers that trembled—clumsy, impatient fingers—he began unbuttoning her blouse. The heat of her skin seared to the center of his being. Finally the soft material parted, baring the ivory mounds of her breasts to his hungry eyes. It took but a second to unhook the front closure of her silky bra and, with a low moan, he eased the lacy cups aside and lowered his head to her sensitive, swollen nipples.

Holly melted at his touch, the gentle massage of his tongue sending currents of desire through her. David teased and taunted first one breast, then the other, until Holly was moaning. He was hot, hungry, male. Wanting her. Needing her. She swayed toward him, boneless and melting. David lifted her into his arms and carried her to the bed, laying her gently on the cover and easing down beside her. In a tangle of arms and legs, he whispered more seductive words in her ear, all the while touching her with hands that knew instinctively how to give the greatest pleasure. Was she capable of making him feel like this?

Holly had never known she could want anyone the way she wanted David at this moment. The way he touched her, the way he looked at her, made her feel as if she were something rare and precious. Rick had never touched her like this. The intimate part of their marriage had been a disappointment to Holly from the beginning. She knew Rick had shared that feeling. He had certainly told her often enough what a dud she was in bed.

For years she had blamed herself for not being able to please him. She had even wondered if she had been better in bed if maybe Rick wouldn't have turned to other women. It had taken her a long time to accept that she wasn't to blame for his infidelities. Now, with the touch of David's hand still warm on her skin, she knew that much of the dissatisfaction of their marriage had been Rick's fault. She had been so naive and innocent when they had married, yet even on their wedding night, Rick had never taken the time to make her feel what she was feeling now. He had never even come close. He had always been too interested in his own gratification to worry about hers. Then he had blamed the failure of their lovemaking on her. She couldn't help but wonder if she could satisfy a man as obviously experienced as David. That fear must have shown in her eyes, because he gazed down at her for a long moment.

"Holly, are you sure this is what you want?" The degree to which she responded to his touch still stunned him. One of the things he loved about her was her sweet air of innocence. Yet her response to him was anything but innocent. Beneath that facade breathed a passionate, sensuous woman.

"I don't know if I can satisfy you," she said in a fragmented whisper.

His eyes were dark with understanding. "Fact is, Holly Carol Nichols, you satisfy me very much. Now, making love involves a little technique, but it's nothing that can't be learned. One of the first lessons is touching." His hand moved down the silky skin of her throat, then across the gentle rise of her breasts, before coming to rest on the soft swell of her abdomen. She inhaled a sharp swift breath. This technique he spoke of? He should bottle it and sell it, Holly thought somewhat wildly. He would make a fortune. But then, the whole world would be able to share in this glorious feeling and Holly selfishly wanted to keep it just for the two of them.

As he had the night before, David took her hand and placed it on his chest. "Touch me, Holly."

She did, loving the feel of him, reveling in the muscles rippling beneath her fingertips, the soft sounds from his throat telling her of the pleasure she brought him. She felt the strong rapid beat of his heart. With each breath, with each whispered encouragement, Holly became bolder, finding her greatest pleasure in pleasing him. She was captured as much by his touch and by touching him as by the soft words he whispered in her ear.

Somehow their clothing was shed and they found themselves lying naked in each other's arms. Heated skin against heated skin. Warm breath mingling. Moist lips clinging.

"Then there's tasting," he whispered, nipping the lobe of her ear and then nursing the tiny hurt with his tongue. His lips trailed down the soft curve of her neck, pausing at the throbbing pulse point before moving even farther. The scent of her, mingled with the taste of her satin skin, drove him to the edge of madness.

"David . . ." she murmured, curling her fingers into the thick silk of his hair as he laved her nipple with his tongue, then drew it fully into his mouth. Her fingertips dug into his scalp, holding him close as wave after wave of excitement rocked her. David went from one breast to the other while Holly urged him on with the touch of her hands and the moaning sounds coming from somewhere deep inside her.

He moved lower, circling her navel with the tip of his tongue. He trailed a line of gentle wet kisses across her flat abdomen. Holly murmured in protest when David kissed the smooth inside of one thigh, then the other. Her murmurs turned to gasps of shock when his mouth moved to the very core of her femininity.

"David, please," she begged, not knowing exactly what it was she was begging for. Waves of heat washed through her. Tension built and built inside her until she thought she would explode.

David felt her shudders of release and knew he was fast losing control. She was so responsive it wasn't easy for him to hold back. It had been so long since he had been with a woman. Never had one affected him this way. Always he had been in control. He couldn't quite figure out when he had lost control here. "You certainly are a fast learner," he rasped through clenched teeth. She was teaching him things about touching, caring and intimacy that he hadn't known existed. Her generous giving of herself unlocked something inside of him that he had kept hidden and protected for most of his life, a part of him no woman had ever touched before. The loneliness of his life disappeared in her touch. The vulnerability he had kept hidden from the world opened to her to do with as she may.

When he moved to capture her lips once more, her hand slipped down to cup him intimately and he nearly hurtled over the edge. He caught her hand and held it. "I can't wait any longer, Holly."

Her breath came in ragged gasps. She felt the power of his need for her and, at the same time, felt her own control disappearing. "Now, David," she whispered, arching into him. "Please, love me now."

Slowly, savoring every second, David joined their bodies, burying himself deep inside her. He lay there for a moment, brushing her lips with his while he regained what slender control he had left. Then together in exquisite harmony, they traveled to the stars and beyond, soaring higher and higher until they reached that ultimate peak, then drifted back to earth together.

"I love you, Holly," he whispered, gathering her into his arms. "I love you."

"I love you, too, David." Replete, she lay quietly in his arms, listening to the strong steady beat of his heart. She had never known lovemaking could be like this. "I never thought I would love anyone again. When Rick and I were married, I thought I had found my mate for life. I guess I was pretty naive back then. When it all fell apart, I felt as if my world had ended. I trusted him so thoroughly that I was devastated to discover he had betrayed me. For a long time I wondered if I would ever recover."

David closed his eyes, feeling those creeping fingers of fear once again. Somehow he had to tell her the truth, make her understand why he had deceived her so. Most of all, he had to make her believe how much he loved her.

He couldn't lose her.

8

DAVID LAY AWAKE, staring at the ceiling and dreading the coming sunrise. It was time to pay the piper and he wasn't nearly ready. How in the world could he explain to Holly that he wasn't David Winslow but a man whom she loathed and despised? This hadn't seemed nearly as complicated a few nights ago when he had sat in her office listening to her incredible proposition. Still, he had been crazy to think he could get away with it.

Holly stirred and David rose up on one elbow to gaze down at her. The dim light from the bathroom barely split the darkness of the room, but David could make out her features. He would have to wake her soon if they were to be at the airport in time to catch the early flight. He put his finger to the corner of her mouth and she smiled in her sleep. A wave of tenderness swept over him and he couldn't resist placing a gentle kiss at the corner of her lips.

Holly felt the soft brush of something against her mouth and slowly opened her eyes. It took her but a moment to realize where she was and with whom. Memories of last night swamped her and she felt a rush of warmth.

"Hi, sleepyhead," he said huskily.

"Hi, yourself. Is it time to get up?" She fervently hoped not. The warm length of body stretched out next to her seemed far more appealing than getting out of bed.

"Almost," David replied, nuzzling her neck.

"It's still dark outside."

"It usually is at four in the morning. But our plane leaves in a couple of hours."

Holly curved her body into David's, slipping her arms around him and running her hands over the broad width of his back. "Do we have time for breakfast?"

David groaned. "I should have known! Don't you ever think of anything but your stomach?"

She buried her face in the curve of his shoulder, kissing him with growing fervor. "Stomach? I was thinking of something far more exciting than bacon and eggs."

David chuckled. "Oh, really? Like what?"

She kissed the strong curve of his jaw. "I was thinking more along the lines of ravishing your body."

He hugged her close. "Ravish away," he murmured before taking her lips in the kiss he had wanted all along.

HOLLY SAT at her desk, a file lying open before her and papers scattered about. But Holly's mind wasn't on the file, or the papers, or the upcoming appointment. Memories of last night, and this morning, of the hours she had spent in David's arms, had destroyed her powers of concentration. It almost seemed like a dream, but her body still felt the lingering effects of David's passion and Holly knew it was no dream.

A rap sounded on the door and she looked up. "Susan, is Mrs. Armistead here yet?"

"No, she isn't due for another fifteen minutes," Susan told her, glancing at her watch. "Will that give you enough time? I can delay her for a few minutes."

"No, that won't be necessary." She tried again to concentrate on business, to put thoughts of the weekend aside. "All we're going to do is discuss a defined benefit plan. It's only been a few months since her husband died so I don't want her worrying about pensions and such. She has enough to do running that catering business."

Fifteen minutes later, while Holly was going over a list of financial figures to present to Beatrice Armistead, the telephone rang. She picked up the receiver and said, "If Mrs. Armistead is here, Susan, send her right in."

There was pause, then, "Hi, funny face."

Holly's pulse leaped. "David!" Her exclamation of surprise brought a low laugh.

"That's a good sign. You remember my name."

"I'm not likely to forget it."

"I hope not." David paused. "You haven't forgotten anything else, have you?"

Holly drew in a deep breath. Hearing that husky voice brought back vivid memories of him making slow, sensual love to her. "No," she managed to say. "I haven't forgotten one single detail."

"I have to see you, Holly." There was a thread of tension in his voice. "There's something I have to talk to you about."

"Sounds important," she said lightly in an attempt to cover her own sudden tension. "Let me look at my schedule."

"Damn your schedule!"

"David!"

He let out a breath in exasperation. "I'm sorry. It's just that . . . oh, hell! Are you free for lunch?"

Holly hesitated, concerned by David's vehemence. What could be so important it couldn't wait? Susan had told her the schedule was light today. Maybe she could meet David for lunch. She glanced at her calendar and swore silently. Susan had penciled in an appointment at noon. "David, I'm sorry, I can't." Holly caught her lower lip between her teeth when he swore viciously under his breath. "How about dinner at my house? Say, seven?"

David was silent for a long drawn-out moment. "How long will your noon appointment take? Can I see you for a few minutes afterward?"

"I don't know for sure, and there's that meeting at one. I can't guarantee anything except dinner at my house tonight."

He drew in his breath. "I'll be there, no matter what happens. And, Holly—"

Mrs. Armistead opened the door and stepped into Holly's office. "I have to go, David. My client is here."

"I love you, Holly. Remember that."

Holly hung up the phone, more troubled by the call than she wanted to admit, but she had no time to deal with it at the moment.

ACROSS TOWN, David settled back in his chair, his forehead creased in a frown. Nothing had gone right since he left Holly that morning. John had been waiting for him when he arrived at the office, ready to out-

line what D. W. Branson was to say at the meeting that
afternoon with the tenants in Holly's building.

"Bran, you're looking unusually fit this morning."
John's perceptive blue eyes bored into David's. "The
weekend must have agreed with you."

Agreed with him? Yes, David thought, you could say
that. A night and morning of very thorough loving did
that for a man. He moved to the window and stared
out, thinking it had been a lifetime since he stood at this
same window wondering about a fire-breathing dragon
named H. C. Nichols.

An urgent, uncontrollable need for her shot through
him. A need for the taste and scent of her, for the soft
touch of her hands on him. He saw again the warmth
and need in her soft tawny eyes. Trusting eyes.

Despair—cold, black and deadly—knifed through
him. He would lose her. He was sure of it. That cer-
tainty chilled him to the bone. The thought of a future
without her—

"Bran?"

He turned to look at John in surprise. He had forgotten for a moment that he wasn't alone. "I'm sorry,
John," he said in what he hoped was a fairly normal
voice. "My mind was somewhere else."

John's eyebrows rose in question but Bran might as
well have been wearing a sign that said HANDS OFF
in capital letters. "How did your meeting with Ms.
Nichols go?" he asked cautiously.

Holly. Warm and loving, hot and passionate, open,
honest, giving. David shook his head slightly, focus-
ing on John with a determination that caused a tight
knot of tension to form between his shoulder blades.

Maybe he should tell John exactly—well, almost exactly—what had happened between himself and Holly. John was his best friend. But despite their long-standing friendship, he had the feeling even John would draw the line at this.

With stubborn, rigid control, David bit back the words of confession. This was a problem he would have to deal with himself.

"We didn't get much settled," he said at last, avoiding John's direct gaze.

"I take it Ms. Nichols was not receptive to your peacemaking efforts."

David closed his eyes, remembering just how receptive she was, how she had opened to his touch. He shook his head, both to clear it of Holly's image and in answer to John's question. Knowing he had to get John off the subject of Holly, he crossed the room and settled himself in his chair behind the desk. "Did anything happen while I was gone that we should talk about?" He looked up to meet John's piercing, questioning gaze.

"Why don't *you* tell *me*?"

David flinched. If he was being that obvious he might as well tell John the truth. He would find out soon enough anyway. But something held him back. "Don't push this, John." His voice was firm and final.

John held his gaze for a long moment, then reached for his briefcase, opened it and extracted a handful of papers. When he spoke again, his voice was all business. "There's another delay at the civic center. The electrical contractor received a botched-up shipment and it'll be another week to ten days before they can get it straightened out."

David felt the familiar tension creeping in. Sometimes he wondered if the civic center would be finished in his lifetime. If things kept on the way they were going, he would be faced with another lawsuit, this one for breach of contract if the center wasn't finished on time. Damn! He had half a dozen other projects in various stages of development and all of them together didn't give him the headaches this one did.

The rest of the morning tested his patience even further. It seemed that everyone in Indianapolis required his immediate attention, although he managed to squeeze in a haircut between phone calls. By the time he had enough free time to call Holly, he was on the verge of panic.

Now, as his eyes rested on the phone, he was gripped by a sense of frustration. He reached up to run his fingers through hair that was a lot shorter and much better tamed than it had been for some time. There were so many things he needed to do, but he didn't have a clue as to where to begin. He wanted to see Holly. He needed to concentrate on the civic center. He hadn't given it more than a passing thought over the weekend. The only thing he seemed capable of concentrating on at the moment was Holly. He had to see her, to try to explain his actions, and he had to do it before that meeting.

THE VAGUE, indefinable uneasiness that had settled over Holly during David's call lingered long after she hung up the phone. It took all her powers of concentration to present her benefit plan to Mrs. Armistead with any amount of intelligence and coherence. She kept hearing the note of urgency and frustration that had been in David's voice. Something was going on that she knew nothing about and it was making her very nervous.

"I seem to remember reading somewhere that D. W. Branson bought this building, Holly. Is that right?"

Holly forced a smile and nodded her head. "Several months ago."

"What a darling boy he is," the older woman said in an adoring voice.

Holly's head came up and she stared at Beatrice Armistead in surprise. There was an almost-angelic quality about the tiny woman that fully disguised a core of solid steel. With her snow-white hair, twinkling blue eyes and petal-soft skin, she was the image of the perfect grandmother. She was all that and more. Ten years ago, at the age of fifty, she began cooking for friends in the kitchen of the home she shared with her husband of more than thirty years. Her business had grown to be one of the most exclusive and sought-after catering services in Indianapolis. This petite sixty-year-old had more spunk and energy than many women half her age. Holly loved her dearly.

But "darling"? It wasn't exactly a term she would apply to D. W. Branson.

The doubt in Holly's eyes didn't deter Mrs. Armistead one bit. "Bran built our house for us. He always told me I could make a fortune with my cooking."

Bran? It sounded like a breakfast cereal.

"You've known him a long time?" Holly asked politely.

"Ever since he bought that barn of a house he lives in. It's amazing the things he's done with it." Her eyes sparkled with admiration and affection. "I was so glad to see that boy become such a success. No one deserves it more than him. And to take care of his family the way he has! I used to do a little housekeeping for him when the kids were still small. The hours he had to work, it's a miracle those kids turned out as well as they did."

Holly barely listened, writing figures and estimates in Mrs. Armistead's file while trying not to seem rude. She had to admit to a bit of curiosity about this family of Branson's. She didn't know he had ever been married.

"Well, Holly," Mrs. Armistead stated as she got to her feet, "I know you're busy, so I'd better go. I have another appointment in a half hour or so."

Holly rose and walked with her to the door. "I'll call you sometime next week with the final figures. Thank you for coming in today and bringing all that information."

The tiny woman reached up and patted Holly's cheek affectionately. "I can tell something is troubling you, young lady. Don't worry so much. You'll have lines soon enough. And I'm sure that whatever the problem is, you'll work it out. Take care now."

Holly closed the door after her and leaned with her back against it, wondering what dear Mrs. Armistead would say if she knew what Holly's problem was, that all she could think about was a certain David Winslow and how many hours loomed before she would be in his arms again.

She managed to make it through her next appointment with a modicum of professional expertise, then, to her surprise and Susan's, two more clients showed up during lunch hour. Evidently the temporary had managed to confuse the appointment book even more than Holly had first thought. She wondered if the rest of the week was going to be like this. Of course, the confusion had left her little time to think about David or to fret about the fast-approaching meeting with D. W. Branson.

At a few minutes to one, Susan stuck her head in the door and told Holly she was going out to pick up some sandwiches. After she left, Holly cleared her desk, preparing to leave for the meeting. On her way out, she stopped at Susan's desk to double-check her schedule for the remainder of the day. Of course she had no idea how long the meeting with Branson would take. Looking down at the appointment book, Holly saw that Susan had marked out the time until three-thirty.

The outer door opened and Holly looked up, startled when a young man stepped inside. Dressed in Levi's and a black leather jacket, he carried a motorcycle helmet under his arm. Thick ebony hair curled below his collar and he sported a heavy beard. It was difficult to judge his age, but she guessed him to be somewhere in his midtwenties.

Holly's first thought was that he might be another unscheduled appointment; the next was that there was something vaguely familiar about him. This second thought kept her from feeling any fear, despite the man's untamed looks. That, and the fact that she had been around motorcycles and the people who rode them for most of her life.

"Hello," he said. "I'm looking for D. W. Branson and you seem to be the only one around. Do you know where I might find him?"

Holly frowned. "No, I don't." She stared at the man, wondering why he would think she knew Branson's whereabouts and what it was about him that bothered her so.

He gave her an engaging smile and took another step into the room. "I'm sorry to disturb you, but may I use your phone? I just got in from out of town and was told I could find my brother at this address—that he has a meeting in this building. I'd like to call his secretary and see if she knows what time he'll be here."

"One o'clock."

"Pardon me?"

"The meeting is at one o'clock."

He glanced at the clock on the wall behind Holly. "It's one o'clock now." He gestured toward the phone. "May I?"

Holly nodded, marveling at his persistence. Hadn't she just told him the meeting was at one? He appeared to be as arrogant and overbearing as his brother.

The young man stepped up to the desk and perched on the edge, reaching for the telephone. As he punched in the numbers, he cradled the receiver on his shoulder, then turned to give Holly another beguiling smile. His eyes were dark, as green as a forest glade in summertime. Holly felt a quiver of some undefined dread trickle down her spine.

"Hello, Fran? This is Nick."

Holly went very still. Even the blood seemed to slow in her veins.

"I'm at the office building you said to come to, but I can't find David anywhere. Have you heard from him?"

9

HOLLY PALED. She dropped into the chair behind Susan's desk and sat there, staring in shock at the young man.

"He did?" Nick looked over at Holly and frowned. "Okay, I'll wait for him here. Thanks, Fran." He replaced the receiver, his eyes still on Holly. "Are you all right, ma'am?"

No wonder he disturbed her, she thought a little wildly. Except for the long hair and beard, he looked the way David might have looked ten years ago.

"Ma'am?"

Holly gazed up at him, taking a long unsteady breath before she tried to speak. "I . . . I'm fine. I was just— thinking of something else."

Nick stood, staring down at her with a slight frown. "Thanks for letting me use your phone," he said after a moment.

"You're welcome," she said in a choked voice.

He straightened and moved toward the door. "Well, thanks again. I'll wait for my brother outside. His secretary said he should be here any minute. Maybe I'll see you around."

"Maybe not," Holly muttered as she watched him pull the door shut behind him. This had to be a dream. She'd fallen asleep at her desk and would wake up any minute to find this entire incident was a dream—a crazy nightmare.

David Winslow is D. W. Branson?

Holly shook her head in denial. It couldn't be true. It was a coincidence.

Right, Holly, she derided herself. David Winslow and D. W. Branson both have a black-haired, green-eyed younger brother named Nick. And pigs flew and hell froze over just last week.

Slowly Holly rose to move toward the door on unsteady legs. She had to know. She had to see the proof for herself.

She opened the door and started to step out into the hallway when she saw them. They stood just inside the building entrance not more then twenty feet from her. Two men, so alike and yet so different. One stood tall and lean, dressed in a tailored suit of charcoal silk, his ebony hair precision-cut and tamed within an inch of its life. The other man faced him, just as lean but not quite so tall, dressed in jeans and a leather jacket.

Brothers.

The taller man, the one who had to be D. W. Branson himself, turned toward her, his eyes widening in shock as he gazed at her across the distance that separated them. David—her David—looked at her with eyes shadowed with pain, regret and . . . what? A plea for forgiveness?

Holly stepped back into her office and shut the door. It couldn't be true. It just couldn't. As if in a trance, she went into her own office and crossed to the window. She didn't know how long she stood there. It could have been hours or only minutes, but the next thing she heard was Susan's voice.

"Holly, what happened? Is the meeting over already? It's only two o'clock."

Holly didn't turn around, just continued to stare sightlessly out the window. "I didn't go."

"Why not? Did Branson cancel again?"

Shock gave way to disbelief, then humiliation and finally rage. Not even with Rick had she felt so totally, so thoroughly betrayed.

"That bastard! That low-down lying bastard!" Holly's voice trembled with an anger that kept the pain and humiliation at bay. "I could strangle him."

Susan made a slightly choked sound. "Uh—Holly."

"I could! If I had Mr. D. W. Branson Development, Incorporated here right now, I'd strangle him with my bare hands," Holly ranted. "I'd make him sorry he ever tried to play me for a fool."

"Holly!" Susan's voice took on a warning note.

"It's all right, Susan. I'll handle it from here."

At the sound of David's voice, Holly spun around, stunned into speechlessness. Susan was just stepping out, and he stood with his back to the door, hands shoved into the pockets of his tailored trousers, the corners of his mouth lifted in a smile that didn't quite reach his eyes. All she could do was stare at the implacable features of the man who was obviously amused at her humiliation.

"That's a switch from the things you wanted to do to my body this morning." His lids were lowered to hide the pain and wariness in his eyes. He was at a loss as to how to salvage the situation.

Crimson flags of color stained Holly's cheeks as she struggled for control. "How dare you!" she spat, her fury nearly choking her. "How dare you make a remark like that after what you've done."

David felt as if he were crossing a field dotted with land mines. It was all he could do to assume a casual stance, to keep the corners of his mouth lifted in a smile and to meet her furious gaze with a steadiness that belied the feeling of helplessness trapping him. His first thought was to bluff his way through. Then he thought better of it. Hadn't he known all along it would come to this? He had been on a collision course with this moment from the first. It didn't stop the pain, though. He would do anything to wipe that look of disillusionment and betrayal from her face.

Taking a deep ragged breath, Holly fought the urge to hurl something at him, something large and heavy or sharp and lethal. Anything to knock that smile off his face. "What have you done?" The question was a bare whisper. "Is this your idea of fun? You have the nerve to warn me about perverts when you have the most perverted sense of humor I've ever encountered? Was answering that ad your little joke for the week?"

"I didn't answer your ad, Holly."

Searching his face—his dear, beloved, stranger's face—Holly clenched her hands into tight fists, her fingernails digging into the soft flesh of her palms. "What are you saying?"

"When I walked into this office, I wasn't aware of any ad," he went on.

He sounded so calm, so reasonable. Confusion, disbelief and doubt twisted Holly's features. "You canceled your appointment that night. What possible reason could you have had for being here?" She tried to associate this faultlessly attired, self-possessed business tycoon with a jeans-clad David Winslow playing touch football in the park in Valentine. How had that unruly mass of ebony hair suddenly become so relentlessly well tamed? Obviously when one could afford to pay a king's ransom for a haircut, miracles were possible.

Easing away from the door, David moved toward her, a shaft of pain shooting through him when he saw the startled fear in her eyes. "I didn't cancel that appointment, Holly," he said carefully. "I came here that night to talk with you about my decision to tear this building down, to apologize for not answering your letters—"

"And to talk me out of a court injunction," she interrupted bitterly. "Did you think my going to bed with you would change that?"

David's jaw clenched. "I didn't come here with the idea of taking you to bed. All I wanted was to try to straighten out the mess I'd made."

"Well, you did a fine job of that, didn't you!" she accused. "Why didn't you tell me who you were?"

"You didn't give me a chance. It took me a while to realize you had no idea who I was. You really threw me a curve when you called me David. No one outside of my family had called me that for years. Before I knew what was happening, I was the other half of a rather interesting business proposition."

"Then what happened to the David who was supposed to be here?" She glared at him as if he were somehow responsible for the absent man's sudden demise.

David shrugged. "I have no idea, but does it really matter? Within five minutes of entering this office, I was glad he'd stood you up."

Holly's anger deepened. "That would have thrown a monkey wrench into your little game, wouldn't it, to have the real David show up? Did you enjoy yourself, Mr. D. W. Branson? After all the beautiful, refined women you've had, it must have been difficult adjusting to a nutso like me! Good for laughs, huh? Did you chuckle your way through the Big Macs and the video games? And how about the charming little homespun weekend in Valentine, Nebraska? That must have bowled you over with merriment!"

Humiliation clawed at her, the pain making serious inroads into her fury. This couldn't be happening. Any minute she would awaken from this nightmare and find that the man she'd given her heart and soul to was not the ruthless D. W. Branson. It just wasn't possible! If the bottom ever fell out of the construction and real estate market, he could make his next million in Hollywood. The man had already earned his first Academy Award with this faultless performance. And she deserved one for being the world's prime fool!

"Holly..." David took another step toward her. Somehow he had to make her understand that he had never meant to hurt her.

She stepped back, holding up her hands to halt his advance. "Don't touch me, Mr. Branson," she warned in a low voice. "It's been great fun, but a weekend I'd just as soon forget. And make no mistake, I will forget

it in time, probably by tomorrow. These little come-
dies have a way of disappearing as quick as can be—
like a joke you hear and then forget the punch line. I'm
sure you have more important things to do with your
valuable time than to reminisce about a weekend that
never happened."

David's eyes flared into emerald fire. "Damn it,
Holly, stop it!" Covering the distance between them in
several long, effortless strides, he imprisoned her
shoulders in a viselike grip. "I told you I wasn't looking
for a one-night stand with you. I meant it. I'm not about
to let you walk out of my life."

Panic rose in Holly at the first contact with his lean,
hard body. . . that body she remembered so well. The
heat of his stong hands burned her flesh just as the fire
in his eyes burned her soul. She brought her hands up
to push against his chest and was swamped by memories of his warm skin beneath her fingertips, of the dark,
curling hair on his chest brushing against her bare,
sensitive breasts. The expensive suit, vest and silk shirt
he wore were no barrier to the familiar frame they covered. Steeling herself against the hunger sweeping
through her, Holly fought to retain her anger and
thereby her sanity.

"Don't you understand, Mr. D. W. Branson?" she
snapped. "It was a fantasy! A fairy-tale fantasy! The
entire weekend was a lie from beginning to end. It
wasn't real!"

"No!" David's hot denial sprang from his lips as his
rigid control shattered. Hauling her against him, he
wrapped his arms around her, trapping her. "Would

you have carried out your little scheme if I had told you who I was?"

"Of . . . of course not!" Holding herself rigid, she fought her body's traitorous response to his touch. She couldn't—wouldn't—allow herself to be drawn into this man's web.

"No, you wouldn't have, and I wouldn't have been able to get near you, Holly, because you would never have allowed it. You're so wrapped up in your preconceived ideas of who and what I am that I wouldn't have stood a chance." His voice dropped to a low, husky whisper that sent frissons of awareness across her nerve ends. "The weekend was no farce, Holly." She squirmed in his arms, but he only tightened his hold. "It was the first real thing to happen to me in a very long time. I fell in love with you, and *that* is real, as real as the man standing here holding you. The man you fell in love with."

Holly inhaled swiftly, sharply. "I fell in love with David Winslow—a man who doesn't even exist."

"Oh, he exists all right, and I'm going to prove it," David murmured, molding Holly's body even more firmly against the unrelenting hardness of his. He took her lips in a passionate kiss laced with desperate urgency.

Holly stiffened, refusing to allow him to break down her reserve. The arms holding her were D. W. Branson's arms and she fought the allure of his muscular body with all the mental powers she possessed. But it was David Winslow's mouth tasting hers with an insistent hunger that took her breath away. His mouth moved over hers and Holly's resistance ebbed and faltered as the world rocked beneath her feet. Gently he coaxed her lips to soften and part, to welcome the exploring tip of his tongue as the kiss deepened. With a soft moan, she melted into the strength of his lean muscular body, the same body she had explored so intimately before dawn.

Finally, all her resistance gone, she rested warm and pliant in his arms. David lifted his head enough to whisper against her lips. "David Winslow and D. W. Branson are one and the same man, Holly. The man who loves you."

Holly's muddled mind struggled with that statement. All she had heard and read about D. W. Branson came hurtling back. Who was he trying to fool? D. W. Branson and David Winslow were as alike as day and night; prime rib and chopped beef; sugar and saccharin. It was all wrong. She couldn't be in love with D. W. Branson.

"No," she denied out loud, resisting the pull of his magnetic, hypnotic eyes. Lying eyes. "Let me go," she said struggling against the rock-hard strength of his arms. "Please!"

To her surprise and relief, David dropped his hands, muttering a short, graphic oath under his breath. "Would you please leave?" she asked quietly.

"Are you denying what's between us, Holly?" A muscle flexed in his jaw.

Moving away from him, Holly refused to meet his eyes. "There is nothing to deny, Mr. Branson. You're very good at destroying people who get in your way. I won't allow you to destroy me." She dared a glance at him. The stricken expression on his face made her falter, but only for a moment. "Your reputation precedes you. Did you think I could forget everything I know about you? I've heard you were ruthless and cold-blooded. I didn't realize how true that was until now. Your cheap seduction tricks may work with all those other women, but you can count me out." His face paled to an ashen gray. Pain clutched at Holly's heart, but she went relentlessly on. "Chalk up that little episode in Omaha to experience. I'm sure with your track record it's just a drop in the bucket." A sharp pain knifed through her even as she said the words. Last night had been so special. At least she had thought so, but he had made it into something cheap and tawdry.

"Do you really believe that garbage you're spouting, Holly?" he asked harshly. Damn, he wanted to shake her! Before she could move, he had once more imprisoned her within his strong arms. His fingers grasped her chin, forcing her to look up at him. "You say you know me? Well, you're right about that! You know me better than anyone else. You know the man behind the image—an image I neither asked for nor wanted. I did what I had to do to survive. If that meant putting someone out of business who was too inept to be there in the first place, I did that, too. It's up to you to determine the truth. If you think I'm going to stand around waiting for you to make up your mind, you're sadly mistaken." He bent his head, taking her mouth for a brief but thorough kiss. "I intend to do everything in my power to sway your thinking in the right direction. I can't lose you, Holly. I won't!"

Holly managed to twist out of his grip and shot him a scathing look. "Get out of here. Now. Get out of my

office and get out of my life. I don't need you." She
jerked the sapphire ring from her finger and flung it at
him. It bounced off the middle of his chest and fell to
the carpet. She turned her back to him, willing him to
leave.

The instant she heard the door close, Holly squeezed
her eyes shut and fought for control. She would not allow him to affect her. She wouldn't! Slowly she moved
to the couch and sank into the deep cushions, feeling
as if she had been run over by a freight train.

"Holly, are you all right?" Susan had come in to sit
down next to her and put a supporting arm around her
shoulders.

Holly turned her head slightly, her flesh pale and
waxen, her eyes as wide and dark as a frightened doe's.
"I...I'm fine," she said in a shaky voice, then closed her
eyes and inhaled deeply. "No, I'm not fine. I think I'll
go home. If I have any more appointments this afternoon, cancel them." She stood on unsteady legs, bending down to retrieve her purse from under the edge of
the couch. She felt as though she were swimming
underwater. Everything had a hazy unreal quality to
it.

Holly turned to say something to Susan, astounded
to discover her eyes filling with unbidden tears. Damn,
she wasn't going to cry. D. W. Branson wasn't worth it.

David Winslow was.

Holly fought the insidious, creeping pain. She had
to get home.

"Do you want me to take you?" Susan asked.

Holly stood straighter, blinking back the telltale tears
and shaking her head. "I'll be fine," she lied, wonder-

ing if she would ever be okay again. She turned tortured, glistening eyes to Susan. "I'm sorry," she whispered. "I just need to be . . . alone for a while."

HOLLY'S ANGER slowly gave way to doubt and confusion as the day slipped into evening. Curled up in the corner of the couch, listening to the low rumble of distant thunder, she wondered if this mess could ever be worked out.

An image of D. W. Branson rose, unbidden, to fill her mind's eye. He was the epitome of self-possession and power: the neatly trimmed, relentlessly obedient ebony hair; the cool, direct green eyes; the fabulous body clothed in a tailor-made suit.

Then there was the other image. It embodied the same self-confidence but was gentler, less rigid. Tousled black hair gleamed like satin in the Nebraska sunshine; devilish green eyes teased and laughed, bold and sensuous. And the lean muscular body was clad in Levi's and well-worn T-shirts; or clad in nothing, and responded to her touch with a fire and passion that even now had the power to send the blood rushing through her veins like molten lava. A man who was tender, gentle, funny and loving. A man whose deep husky voice whispered words of love and encouragement in her ear, leading her to heights of desire she'd never known existed. A man like David.

Which image was true? Which false?

Confusion and doubt assailed her, trapping her. How could she ever forgive him?

Yet, when she thought back to the night he appeared at her office, she had to admit the truth of what he said.

From the moment she'd looked up and seen him standing in the doorway, he hadn't had a chance. And that temporary secretary had been there that day. Chances were she'd canceled the wrong appointment.

When Holly took a long, honest look at their conversation that night, she could see she hadn't given David much of a chance to say anything. She'd been too afraid he was going to back out. He had tried to interrupt several times, but she hadn't allowed it.

Her face flushed hotly at the memory of the things she had said and done with him. She had taken D. W. Branson to McDonald's and fed him Big Macs and french fries, for crying out loud! No wonder he hadn't been to McDonald's for years! He probably enjoyed a steady diet of prime rib and lobster.

She had teased him about not having had an Orange Julius when his taste probably ran to imported wines, and then she had taken him on a tour of a shopping mall that he had built and probably still owned. Finally, she had subjected him to a video arcade when the chances were good that he had season tickets to the Indianapolis Symphony!

Holly closed her eyes, seeing again David Winslow's triumphant face after beating her at Pac-Man. A warm feeling enveloped her as she remembered the shout of joy erupting from his lips, those same lips that had met hers so briefly in the arcade and gone on to explore every inch of her body in a motel in Omaha.

Why? she wondered, crossing her arms over her knees and resting her forehead on them. Why would he deceive her so? Did he really expect her to believe that D. W. Branson would be attracted to someone like her?

Despite a hard-earned self-esteem, Holly was honest about her own limitations. She was attractive and worked hard at emphasizing her attributes, but she knew she would never be classified as a raving beauty. She would never stop traffic on a busy downtown street—not unless her VW broke down in the middle of rush hour. D. W. Branson was notorious for his addiction to beautiful young women who could just as easily grace the cover of a fashion magazine as the society pages of the Indianapolis papers. Holly was just not the glamorous type.

The sound of thunder brought her out of her reverie. Holly lifted her head and looked around, surprised by how dark it had become for so early in the evening. The thunder—no, not thunder this time. Someone was pounding on her front door.

Holly rose from the couch and crossed to the front window, lifting the drapery aside to peer out into the darkness. A sudden flash of lightning illuminated a dark form on the porch.

David.

It took every ounce of willpower she possessed to keep from rushing to the door and letting him in.

DAVID GAZED at the whiskey swirling in his glass and pondered the idea of getting roaring drunk.

The weather matched his mood perfectly. Thunder rumbled, lightning flashed and a driving wind whistled and moaned with resounding fury against the old house.

Thoughts of Holly haunted him until he was convinced he would go mad. Memories of her tawny eyes, warm with passion, mingled with visions of the pain he had caused her. She wouldn't even see him. He had stopped by her house earlier to find it dark and closed against him. He knew she was home. Her car was parked in her driveway, but no amount of pounding on the front door had affected her.

He leaned his head against the back of the couch and closed his eyes, seeing once again her confusion and hurt. He ached with wanting, trying to hold the loneliness at bay so that he could think clearly enough to devise a plan to win her back. He rubbed his eyes in an attempt to erase her image, but nothing seemed to work. Oh, how she haunted him! He remembered in vivid detail every moment of their night in Omaha. Once again he tasted the sweetness of her breasts, felt her velvet warmth encasing him.

His body hardened in reaction to his erotic thoughts and he stood abruptly, swearing viciously under his breath as he hurled his glass into the darkened fireplace. The sound of shattering glass faded in an onslaught of thunder and wind.

"David."

He spun around, startled. "Nick! I didn't know you were here."

"Are you all right?"

David ran a hand through his hair, avoiding Nick's eyes. "Yeah, sure. I'm fine."

"Throwing glasses into the fireplace is a new evening ritual since I left?"

David shook his head. "Did you get settled in all right?"

Nick nodded. "It didn't take long. After I unpacked I lay down for a while and must have dozed off." He scrubbed at his eyes with the heels of his hands, then went to the bar and removed a Coke from the refrigerator. He opened it and took a long swallow before speaking. "David, I'm not going back to college."

I don't need this, David thought, reaching up to dig his fingertips into his nape. He went to the bar and poured himself another drink, wondering if this, too, would end up in the fireplace. He rested his arms on the bar, gazing at Nick with a mixture of anger and disappointment. It had been difficult not to spoil this youngest brother, who had been barely six when their parents died. David had tried to be part-time father, part-time brother and full-time friend to Nick since he'd collected him from a foster home just after Nick's thirteenth birthday.

"Why not?" he asked at last, determined to hold his temper while at the same time wanting to shake some sense into him. He would have given anything at Nick's age for the opportunity to go to college. Instead, he had spent those years building a fledgling business and rebuilding a scattered family.

"I'm not cut out for it, David. College was always your dream, not mine."

David started to protest, but the words died on his lips. He hated admitting it, but Nick was right. If there was one regret he had in his life, at least up until today, it was that he hadn't been able to manage college. Oh, he had taken a few classes here and there, and if he had to do it all over again, he would do it the same way.

"Okay, Nick, I'll concede that point, but the fact remains that you need a college education to make it in this world. I still think it's important."

"Look how far you've come without it."

"Damn it, Nick! We're talking about you, not me! What do you plan to do with the rest of your life? Work at odd jobs until you get enough money together to hit the road on that motorcycle of yours? Is that all you want out of life?"

"No, it isn't," Nick replied somberly. "I'll admit that it's what I've been doing for the past few years, and that I haven't shown you much of a sense of responsibility. But I want to change that, David. That's why I came home."

"How do I know you won't pick up and leave again?" David asked, unable to keep his anger at bay any longer. Yes, he had worried about Nick, every day he had been gone, but he was angry, too. "I mean, pardon me for asking, but I'm sure you can understand if you think about it for a moment."

"David, I'm sorry."

David slammed the glass down on the bar. "Sorry? What are you sorry for, Nick? That you left in the first place? Or that you never found whatever it was you were looking for?"

Nick's jaw tightened in anger. "You're not being fair, David. I know how much you've done for all of us. I don't need to be told. But I want to live *my* life, not yours."

"I wasn't asking you to!"

His hands curled into fists, Nick replied with forced quiet, "Yes, you were." Anger flashed in his eyes. "You wanted me to do all the things you'd never been able to do. I didn't want to go to college. You did. I'm sorry you never got to go, David. Damn, I would give anything if things could have been different. But there's only one thing I've ever really wanted to do, and you've never asked me what it was."

David took a deep calming breath, reluctantly admitting that maybe Nick was right. "All right," he said at last. "I'm asking now."

"I want to work for you."

David was swamped by so many conflicting emotions that for a moment he couldn't speak.

"Why didn't you ever say so?"

"It was never mentioned as an option."

Nick swallowed the rest of his Coke and tossed the can into the trash. Bracing himself against the bar with one hand, he went on earnestly. "Look at it this way, David. All you've ever known is work and raising kids. Isn't it time you had a life of your own? After all, you're not getting any younger."

David reached for the whiskey bottle and splashed more of the liquor into a glass. At the rate he was going, he would really tie one on. He looked over at his younger brother. "Just what do you propose I do to ward off this encroaching senility?"

Nick grinned, pointing at David's glass. "The first thing you can do is lay off the booze. It isn't good for you."

David glanced at the whiskey, then at Nick. He picked up the glass, leaned over the bar and poured the contents in the sink. "Okay, boss, what next?"

Nick's expression was serious. "Hire me, David. Teach me all you know and let me take some of the burden."

"What did you have in mind?"

Nick took a deep breath, then grinned. "Oh, I thought a partnership would be nice. I could live at your condo downtown so I'd be out of your hair. I'll need a Porsche to keep the ladies happy and an expense account to keep *me* happy."

"Is that all?" David asked drily. "I might consider something more along the lines of a skateboard, an allowance and a pup tent at one of the sites."

His brother's eyes brightened. "You mean you'll do it? You'll give me a job?"

"There are conditions, Nick."

"Like what?" Nick's eyes were wary.

"You'll start at the bottom. I'll talk to Jake tomorrow about taking you on. He's the best foreman in the state and can teach you more than any ten men I know. Then I want you to enroll in some courses at the university this fall."

Nick groaned. "David . . ."

"Hear me out, Nick. There are some things Jake and I can't teach you. If you're serious about helping me, you'll need to take some architectural and engineering courses. You can take them at night if you want, or go a couple or mornings a week and work the rest of the time."

He watched a myriad of expressions play across Nick's face and mentally crossed his fingers. He had never thought Nick would want to work with him. It was something he'd never dared dream about, which disturbed him, for he should have seen it in the young boy who had always begged to go to the construction sites with him.

Finally Nick nodded. "All right, I'll do it. I'll do whatever you say."

"Good!" David exclaimed, eyeing Nick's long shaggy hair. "I'll make an appointment for you with my barber first thing tomorrow."

His younger brother laughed. "I was going to suggest it, but somehow I knew you'd beat me to it." His expression grew serious once more. "David, I'm sorry about this afternoon."

"What do you mean?"

Nick shrugged. "I can't help but think I made a big mistake calling Fran from a certain young lady's office."

David's eyes shadowed. "It wasn't your fault, Nick. I have no one to blame for that fiasco but myself."

Nick looked at him for a long moment. "That bad, huh?"

"Yeah."

"You know, it's really a funny coincidence, your buying that particular building."

"Oh? Why is that?"

"Do you remember Patti Bennett, the girl I took to the prom back in high school?"

David nodded, remembering a pretty blonde who had been only one of many adoring females who followed Nick around.

"Her grandfather built that building. He told me one time he still has the original blueprints."

David straightened, his interest fully aroused. "You're kidding!"

Nick shook his head adamantly. "No, I'm not. I visited him a couple of times that summer after graduation. He was in his eighties, but his mind was as clear and sharp as you could ever hope for."

David's mind raced. An idea took shape. Maybe it wouldn't work, David thought, but then again, maybe it would. If so, it would be the ideal solution. "Do you know if he's still alive?"

Nick's smile was wide and full of mischief. "No, but I could call Patti and find out."

David grinned back. "Oh, you could! Well, I'll just let you do that, and if you get the information for me first thing tomorrow, dinner is on me, your choice."

"No problem," Nick assured him. "Well, I think I'll call it a night."

He was almost to the stairs when David called, "Nick . . ." The younger man turned around. "In a year or two," David said with a grin, "we'll talk again about that partnership."

David lay in bed hours later, unable to sleep as he thought about all the possibilities Nick's suggestions opened up. If he could rebuild the building as it had once been, maybe Holly wouldn't be so fanatical in her opposition. He couldn't wait to work out the details. Then he would tell her—if she would let him get close enough to talk. Whatever he did, he just had to find a way to win her back!

10

HE WAS trying to make her crazy.

It was the only answer, Holly thought, gazing in dismay at yet another long white florist's box, which she knew would contain another dozen roses. She had enough already to open her own florist shop. In just two weeks, David Winslow Branson had done everything he could to drive her to distraction.

Today it was roses. Yesterday it had been singing telegrams. The day before that ...

The day before that was Sunday. One week exactly from the night they had spent together in Omaha. She arrived home from church to find her neighbors gathered in her front yard, clustered around a huge sign proclaiming to the world that David Loves Holly. Mortified, she had turned her car around and left, not returning until after dark. The entire neighborhood probably thought she had gone nuts!

Now there were the flowers. Her office smelled like a funeral home. Red roses, white roses, yellow roses, pink and lavender roses—roses of every color and variety filled the two rooms. The tables, desks, file cabinets, credenzas, even the floor, held roses and more roses.

Each delivery had an accompanying message: "I love you."

Holly wondered when it would end. She found it difficult to get any work done with the constant interruptions. On the other hand, there was something infinitely endearing about a man like D. W. Branson spending so much time ordering flowers. Maybe he really did love—

She shook her head. It would never do for her to think that way. She finally told Susan not to accept any more deliveries.

There was a knock on the door and Holly closed her eyes in frustration. Susan was out to lunch and she would be willing to bet there was another delivery man at her door. Rising, she crossed the room and jerked the door open, determined to put a stop to this once and for all.

Ronald McDonald stood in the doorway, his painted smile broadening at the sight of her.

I don't believe this, Holly thought, clamping her lips together to keep from laughing.

"Yes, sir, may I help you?" she asked with a perfectly straight face.

He handed her two sacks with the familiar logo on them and backed away, still smiling but silent.

Holly closed the door and leaned against it. She didn't have to look in the sacks to know what they contained. Swallowing the urge to laugh, she suddenly felt hot tears stinging the backs of her eyes. She couldn't help it, her body shook with sobs.

HOLLY DIDN'T HEAR any more from David for the rest of the week. She drove home Friday night tired but dreading the long weekend. Try as she might, Holly found it nearly impossible to forget him. Working twelve hours a day hadn't helped. At any time of day and night—it didn't seem to make much difference—an image of him would plague her, haunting her until she couldn't think or work. She tossed and turned half the night remembering the heat of his passion and the way he could make her tremble with a mere touch. She hadn't had a decent night's sleep since Omaha.

Her appetite wasn't worth a damn, either. She must have lost five pounds since she came home from Valentine. How long could a human exist without food or sleep? And Ronald McDonald paid her a visit every day at lunchtime. Even he couldn't entice her to eat.

She pulled into the driveway and shut off the ignition, then rested her forehead on the steering wheel and sighed in despair. She had approximately sixty hours on her hands and for the life of her she couldn't think of one thing to do to fill them. Had her life always been this empty? If she was lucky, this was all a passing phase.

Phase, hell! she thought, getting out of the car. This was more like a life sentence.

She found the source of her impending breakdown on her porch swing when she climbed the steps a few minutes later.

"What are you doing here?" she demanded. This would all be so much easier if she could stop wanting him. She tried not to care about the dark shadows smudging his eyes or the fact that there was more silver at his temples. Could hair turn gray in two weeks?

David grasped the arm of the porch swing, fighting the urge to haul her into his arms. It seemed an eternity since he'd held her. She'd lost weight. Not much, but on her small frame it was easily detected. "I've come to take you to dinner. You obviously haven't been eating the lunches I've sent you."

"Dinner?" Holly stared at him as if he had just landed from Mars. Lord, she was tempted. Maybe a few hours with him would cure her. Then again, maybe it would just make her crazier. To her surprise, and without any prompting from her brain, her mouth said, "Okay. Just give me a few minutes to get ready."

David was so shocked he could only nod his head and follow her into the house. It had been too easy. He couldn't help but wonder what she was up to.

The restaurant he selected was tucked away in the corner of a recently renovated warehouse. It was dark, intimate and very Italian with red-checked tablecloths and candles stuck in Chianti bottles. The aroma of cheese, garlic and sausage made Holly's stomach rumble and her mouth water.

The waiter led them to a secluded corner table, and after they were seated, David ordered a bottle of wine while Holly opened the menu, nearly fainting when she saw the prices.

"I haven't had much of an appetite lately," she mumbled after the waiter left. "I really don't know what I want."

"Would you like me to order for us?"

She nodded and laid the menu aside with a sigh of relief. If she didn't have to make any decisions, she wouldn't feel guilty about how much it cost. She looked at the man seated across from her and almost laughed.

Why should she worry about cost when he could afford to buy the restaurant?

David ordered tossed salad and fettuccine with white clam sauce. The wine was excellent and conversation was kept to a minimum until the food arrived. Holly took one sniff and found her appetite returning in full force. Then she tasted the clam sauce and decided it was probably the most exquisite tasting food she had ever put in her mouth. She dug in with relish.

"I thought you didn't have much of an appetite."

She looked up to see David smiling indulgently and her heart did a traitorous little flip-flop. Damn, but he had a wonderful smile.

"You look tired," she said.

He shrugged. "I haven't been sleeping well." Not since Omaha.

"Problems?"

Yes, one in particular, spelled H-o-l-l-y. "The usual." He didn't elaborate, not wanting to go into all the problems at the civic center tonight.

"How is Nick?" she asked, giving herself a mental pat on the back for being able to so casually bring up a subject that reminded her of one of the most painful days of her life. "Why did he take off like that?"

David picked up his glass and took a sip of the robust wine. Did she have any idea how beautiful she looked with the candlelight giving her skin a golden glow? She wore a simple dress of bright turquoise that enhanced her skin coloring and made her eyes sparkle with golden lights. He wanted to kiss her so badly he could taste it.

He forced his thoughts back to her question and began telling Holly about his talk with Nick and how surprised he had been to find out why his brother had done what he had done.

"Did you get my flowers?"

Holly picked up her glass, eyeing him over the rim. "Are you asking about a particular shipment or would any of the twenty dozen or so do?"

He reached for her hand and raised it to his lips. "I guess I got a little carried away, didn't I."

She nodded, forgetting her irritation with him about the roses. The touch of his warm breath on her fingertips was far more exciting.

They spoke of other things, sharing incidents that had happened during the past week. The waiter came to clear the table, then set dishes of spumoni ice cream in front of them before Holly realized she was actually holding a conversation with the infamous D. W. Branson and thoroughly enjoying it. It unsettled her. She looked at him, thinking that while one appetite had been thoroughly appeased by the delicious food and the invigorating company, an empty place in her still longed to be filled. Unbidden images of his naked body rose in her mind. She could actually feel the heated satin of that same skin with her lips.

David raised his head and saw the fire in her eyes. His body immediately responded and he drew in a long shaky breath. The hand that reached for his wineglass trembled ominously. Lord, how he wanted her.

"Let's get out of here," he said in a tight voice.

Unable to force any words past the lump in her throat, Holly merely nodded. What good would it do to deny her hunger for him? It would be like denying her body's need for food. It seemed to take hours for the waiter to take David's credit card and return with the form for him to sign. Finally he stood and reached for her hand.

Within ten minutes they arrived at a condominium complex, and as David searched for a place to park, Holly couldn't help the feeling of disappointment that swamped her. The complex looked like many others, with row upon row of identical stuccoed units clustered around a swimming pool and clubhouse. How could David live in a place like this? Somehow it just didn't fit.

Maybe she was wrong. Maybe it fit D. W. Branson perfectly.

David parked the Blazer in front of one of the units and got out, coming around to open her door before leading her to the front door of an end unit. He unlocked the door and ushered her inside. "You live here?" she asked, stepping into the elegant living room. It was all silver gray and blue and chrome.

"Nobody lives here, Holly," he explained. "I keep this for entertaining. My home is—my home. I use this mostly for business." He reached for her.

Holly felt the most wonderful sensation flow through her when David's arms went around her and his mouth settled on hers, a warm feeling of homecoming.

The kiss seemed to go on forever, yet when David finally lifted his head, Holly wanted more. Fire burned deep in the emerald depths of his eyes and she wondered if he would take her there, right there on the floor of the entryway. Instead, he grasped her hand and led her up a curving stairway. His bedroom was at the end of a short hallway. After they entered, he closed the door behind them and stood quietly, drinking in the sight of her, his eyes blazing with passion.

"I need you, Holly," he whispered, his low voice raw with desire. "If you only knew the hell I've been through—"

She reached up to touch his lips with her fingertips. "Shh," she whispered, knowing what that hell was like, she had been there, too. With hands that trembled, she began unbuttoning his shirt, feeling the warmth of his skin through the thin fabric. As the shirt slowly parted beneath her fingers, Holly felt the tension rise in David. Finally, slipping her hands under the edges of his shirt, she slowly slid it off his shoulders and it fell to the floor at their feet. Then she reached for the waistband of his slacks.

David began to help her, but she put a hand on his to stop him. "No," she whispered. "Let me." She stretched up to kiss him softly, drawing away when he would have prolonged the kiss.

Holly remembered what he had said that night in Omaha, words whispered in the dark as he explored her body so thoroughly. Words about touching and tasting. Now, as she slowly, provocatively undressed him, she heeded those words, laying a trail of soft kisses across his flat stomach, running her hands over hair-speckled skin and taut muscles. Finally he stood naked before her.

Holly inhaled sharply, unable to tear her eyes from the sight of his lean naked body. Lord, she had forgotten how beautiful, how perfect, he was. She stood rooted to the spot, unable to do anything but run her eyes hungrily over his familiar form. She saw the dangerously hot look in his eyes and felt her blood quicken.

Holly lifted her eyes to his, noticing the rise and fall of his bare chest. It amazed her that she could have such an effect on any man. Her heart stopped, then picked up again with a swift unsteady beat. The blood sang in her veins. She couldn't move, could only watch in fascination as he reached for her. She took in her breath slowly, inhaling his clean masculine scent, then reached out to lay her hand on his chest.

David's fingers wrapped around hers and the breath hissed between his teeth as her other arm curled around his neck and she brought his head down to meet her parted lips.

His arm went around her and he drew her close. The hard evidence of his arousal pressed against her and a hot heaviness began to form in the lower part of her body. His lips were firm and demanding, moving over hers with a hunger that made her weak.

He wanted to love her long and easy, but he couldn't control the clamor of his body. Too many long nights had been spent wanting her. He tried to take it slow and easy when he began to undress her, but his need was too great, his eyes too hungry for the sight of her lovely, naked body. Her soft moans, when he picked her up and carried her to his bed, were almost his undoing. Her hands were as hot and searching as his, her lips every bit as demanding. He wanted to slow down, to savor every delicious inch of her, but not until he was buried deep inside her did he feel any sense of relief. And that lasted for only a fleeting moment before she arched against him and he was lost.

"YOU FELL ASLEEP."

David slowly opened his eyes. Asleep? He thought he had died. The sight that met his eyes almost convinced him he had not only died, he had gone to heaven. Holly sat next to him on the bed, dressed in nothing but one of his T-shirts and holding a cup of steaming coffee.

He sat up, rubbing a hand over his eyes. "What time is it?"

"Almost ten."

That meant he had slept for only about an hour. "Why are all the lights on?"

"The lights aren't on. The sun is shining."

"Come on, Holly, quit kidding around."

She reached up to smooth his hair. It was amazing what thirteen hours of sleep could do for a person. He looked wonderfully rested and sexy and, heaven help her, she wanted him again. There was something infinitely endearing about a sleep-tousled D. W. Branson. "Trust me, David, it's really almost ten—in the morning."

"It can't be! I've never slept this late in my life."

Her eyes sparkled wickedly. "Wore you out, did I?"

He grinned, a slow, sexy grin that took Holly's breath away. "In more ways than one, wench." He marveled at how beautiful she looked. "How long have you been up?"

"Not long." She was entranced by the sight of his bare chest. Memories of last night's wildly passionate lovemaking assailed her. Leaning over, she set the mug of coffee on the nightstand, then turned to face him, feeling the heat rise in her at the slumberous look in his eyes. Standing, she pulled the T-shirt over her head and let it drop to the floor, smiling at the sound of his soft gasp. He was turning her into a wanton, she thought distractedly, bending down to take his lips with hers. How quickly he could make her want him!

David's arms went around her and he pulled her down to sprawl across him, luxuriating in the minty taste of her lips, in the weight of her on top of him. It felt so good to be able to feast on her lovely mouth at leisure, to run his hands slowly over her soft body. He rolled over so that she lay beneath him and clasped her face in his hands. A lazy, sensuous fire burned in her eyes. He bent his head, brushing her lips lightly with his. He had wanted to do this last night, he thought, trailing a line of feather-soft kisses along her cheek and down her neck to the pulse beating at the base of her throat. He let his lips rest there for a moment, absorbing her life's beat before moving down to the softness of her breast.

Holly drew in her breath in anticipation of his intimate touch. Slowly he teased her nipple before drawing it fully into his mouth. She clasped the back of his head, holding him there until she thought she would surely die of the pleasure. She felt hot, burning hot and out of control. Her hands moved restlessly over him, wanting him inside of her while at the same time wanting to revel in the beauty of just touching him and having him touch her.

His fingers trailed over her, followed by his lips, seeking and finding places she had never before thought erotic. With David every touch, every taste was sensual, loving and beautiful.

It was torture, sweet, exquisite torture. She writhed under his touch, moaned when his lips trailed across her sensitive skin, begged him to stop when what she really wanted was for him to go on forever. It seemed like hours, an eternity, before he finally pulled her beneath him and she could welcome him into her body.

"Am I hurting you?"

"No," she managed to say, moving against him.

"Holly."

"More, David," she begged, gripping his buttocks to pull him even deeper inside her. "Please."

"I don't want to hurt you."

"You won't."

"Holly! You feel so good."

"So do you."

He began to move, savoring the joy of loving her slowly and thoroughly. Then the tension began to rise and he knew he was nearing the edge. He shuddered with the force of his climax, holding Holly tightly through her own release. When their breathing finally returned to normal, she lay with her head on his damp chest. He stroked her hair, marveling at how she could so completely satisfy and delight him.

He sighed with contentment. Holly brought so much joy into his life. It was difficult to remember what his life had been like without her in it. Except for the past couple of weeks. That had been sheer hell. But his life had changed so drastically since he had stepped into her office. Had it really been such a short time ago?

It seemed amazing that he could be sleepy again. *Damn*, he thought as he drifted off, *I must be getting old.*

"HOW LONG can a person live on sex?"

"I'm not sure. Has anyone ever done a study on it?"

"Probably."

"Is there anything to eat in this ivory tower?"

"Ivory tower?"

"Food, David. Food."

"There must be something here somewhere. Did you check the freezer?"

"Ice cubes."

"That's all?"

"Unless you count the TV dinner I ate while you slept."

"You didn't."

"I did."

"Pig. Oh, what are you doing?"

"Punishing you for calling me a pig, sleepyhead."

"Ahh, if this is punishment, I'll take a life sentence."

"ARE YOU AWAKE?"

"I'm not sure. Are my eyes open?"

Holly raised up on one elbow. "Can you see me?"

"No."

"Then I guess they're not open. Doesn't that mean you're asleep?"

"I'm not sure."

Holly gave him a playful poke in the ribs. "There's something decadent about sleeping nineteen out of twenty-four hours."

David grinned. "No there isn't. That was essential. Decadent is what we were doing the other five hours." He opened his eyes and looked up at her. "Are you saying we should get up?"

"Do you think you still can?"

David groaned. "That was very tacky, Nichols."

"Don't forget tasteless. Are you going to feed me or do I have to go home to get a decent meal?"

"Is that as opposed to an indecent one?"

"This conversation is going downhill very fast." Holly slid to the edge of the bed. "I'm going to take a shower. During that time I will expect you to do your part in finding this starving body some sustenance, or else." She strode unashamedly naked across the floor to the bathroom door.

"Is that a threat, Nichols?"

"A promise, Winslow."

When Holly emerged from the bathroom nearly forty-five minutes later, the bed was empty. A smile played around her lips as she picked up the oversize T-shirt she had discarded that morning and tugged it over her head. She descended the stairs, the enticing aroma of food beckoning her to the kitchen.

She leaned against the door frame and watched him. He stood with his back to her, clad only in a knee-length, navy blue velour robe. Holly went to him and slid her arms around his trim waist. He turned to kiss her softly on the lips.

"Is my dinner ready yet?" she asked, releasing him and crossing the kitchen to perch on a tall stool at the breakfast bar. She propped her elbows on the counter and rested her chin on the palm of one hand.

"You have a one-track mind, Nichols."

"Two."

He turned around, a heaping plate of food in either hand. "A culinary masterpiece if I ever saw one."

Her eyes met his and she wondered for a moment if he meant the food . . . or her. "You do good work, Mr. Win—David." She stared at the monogram embroidered on the breast pocket of his robe—DWB—then looked quickly away.

He placed the heaping plates of food on the counter and pulled a stool over for himself. His gaze on her was direct and steady. "It still bothers you, doesn't it."

It wasn't a question, and she knew it would do no good to lie to him. "Yes," she said in a low voice.

"I can't change who I am."

Holly straightened, her mouth set in a tight line. "Please, let's not talk about it now." It was much easier for her to deal with the idea of spending the better part of a weekend in bed with David Winslow than with D. W. Branson.

"We're going to have to, sometime."

She dropped her head. "I know." When she lifted it to meet his eyes, her heart leaped in her chest. "Can't we just enjoy what we have right now?" She turned away from the flicker of pain in his eyes. "Maybe I should just go home and forget this ever happened."

His hand closed around her upper arm. "We both tried that, Holly, and it didn't work. What makes you think it will be any different this time? Especially now?"

Now that she had spent most of the past twenty-four hours in his bed? Good question. But, like so many others, one she couldn't answer.

"Holly, I know that with the stories you've read and the things you've heard about me, you're going to find this hard to believe, but I hadn't been with a woman for over a year before that night in Omaha. I hadn't met one that even vaguely interested me." He could tell she didn't believe him. "Not until I met you."

Lord, she wanted to believe him, but it sounded too outlandish to be true. D. W. Branson was definitely not the celibate type. "Why me?"

He cupped her face in his hands, his thumbs gently stroking the corners of her mouth while he took careful inventory of every facet of her small features. Then he said softly, "Beats the hell out of me."

He bent his head and placed a pleading kiss on her mouth. "Stay, Holly, please."

How could she deny him anything when he looked at her like that? "Okay," she said with a ghost of a smile. "I'd hate to see all of this food go to waste."

She climbed back on the stool and picked up her fork. "Speaking of which, just where did you find all this food, anyway? The cupboards were bare when I searched them."

"You just didn't know where to look."

"I looked everywhere."

"The yellow pages."

"Of course."

THE FIRE in the fireplace had burned down to glowing embers. "Do people normally have a fire in the fireplace in May?"

"If it's forty degrees and raining outside."

"It's seventy degrees and clear as a bell."

"But we have the air conditioner on."

Holly turned her head to look at him. His skin was like polished bronze in the firelight. "I guess it's all right then."

David traced the curve of her cheek with his fingertips. "You are so beautiful in the firelight."

She trembled at his touch, musing that she had agreed to have dinner with him only because she thought a few hours with him would cure her. Now she wondered if she would ever be cured. They had made love countless times in the past forty-eight hours and her response was still the same. It frightened her, this power he had over her.

"I need you, Holly," he said huskily. "Sometimes I feel as if my life is spinning out of control and you're the only thing that makes sense, the only thing that gives my life direction."

Holly grasped his hand in hers and raised it to her lips. "David, I asked you once about what happened when your parents died. You avoided the subject. Will you tell me now?"

David hesitated. Turning his head slightly to gaze into the fading embers, he said, "Is it really important? All of that happened so long ago."

"It's important to me," she replied softly.

After a long moment he began to speak. "I was in the car with them—my parents—when the accident happened. I woke up in the hospital a few days later and they were gone, all of them. The state had taken my brothers and sisters and put them in various foster homes. I had just turned sixteen a few months before, so when I got out of the hospital, I went to a foster home, too."

"David, I'm so sorry," she whispered, clasping his hand tightly. "What did you do?"

"I ran away. I knew that if I never did anything else in my life, I would at least get us all back together again. I came to Indianapolis and landed a job on a construction crew. It took a long time, but I finally got enough money together to make a down payment on a house. It wasn't much of a house back then. It was old and run-down, but it was the only thing I could afford and it was big enough for all of us."

He made it sound so easy, Holly thought, but she could see the old pain reflected in his eyes. It wasn't difficult to put two and two together and come up with the parts of the story he wasn't telling her. It couldn't have been as easy as he made it sound to get his family back together again. Not many men would have bothered.

David drew her to him. "I love you, Holly. I can't let you go. You fill an empty place in my life I didn't even know existed. This weekend has been a fantasy I don't want to see end." His lips brushed hers. "I can't seem to get enough of loving you."

11

HOLLY FORCED her eyes open and looked around. It was quiet. Too quiet. Sunlight streamed through the window and she watched the dust motes dancing in the air before she sat up and swung her legs over the edge of the bed. She cocked her head and listened for a sound, any sound other than the noise of traffic outside or the chirping of birds. A jet plane whined overhead. A dog barked. A car horn honked. Other than that, nothing.

He was gone. She knew it even before she picked up his robe and slipped it on to go downstairs, softly calling his name. She knew it before she walked into the startling black-and-white kitchen, where a fresh pot of coffee waited with a note propped against it. *Have an early-morning appointment. Take the car that's in the garage. Will call you later.* She read the note, then eyed the set of car keys warily. He had left her a car? The only thing she had ever seen him drive was the Blazer, and that would be like driving a Mack truck after her VW. But no, he would have taken the Blazer. He must have another car.

She took a cup from the cabinet and filled it with coffee, then stood looking out the window at a cobalt sky and a morning filled with so much sunshine she was tempted to call in sick and just laze the day away. Decadent. That's what it was, she thought. She had lazed enough this weekend to last at least a year.

She had loved enough to want a lifetime.

Her hands went to the smooth silk initials DWB on the pocket of his robe. He had said it still bothered her. He was right. He said they would talk about it. Right again. What he didn't know, but what she would tell him the first chance she got, was that she loved him.

She loved him. Holly sucked in her breath with a soft hiss, then exhaled in a swift rush. She loved D. W. Branson. It was so much easier to admit it than she had thought. Far easier than to keep trying to argue herself out of it. There were things she would have to learn to deal with, ideas and images she'd had about D. W. Branson that she just couldn't reconcile with what she knew about him, really knew about him on a personal, intimate level.

Intimate. Did that word even begin to cover what they had shared? Would life with David Branson—it was the first time she had thought of him with that name—always be as exciting, as fulfilling, as this weekend had been?

Probably not, she thought with a laugh, or they would both be dead inside of a month.

Holly finished her coffee, refilled the cup and carried it upstairs. As she dressed, she wondered when she would see him again. He had said in his note that he would call her. She considered phoning Susan and telling her she'd be late, but a glance at the clock on the nightstand indicated that if she hurried, she could get home and change clothes and still make it to the office on time.

When she opened the door to the garage her mouth dropped open in shock. There sat a bright red Ferrari. A Ferrari? He had to be kidding! Surely, after all he'd had to say about her driving, he couldn't possibly trust her with a car like this! She tried to hide her excitement as she opened the door and settled herself into the luxurious leather seat, wondering if she could ever get used to something like this. A glance at the dashboard almost had her running back inside to call a cab. It looked like the control panel of a jet airliner. She found the ignition and inserted the key. Cautiously she started the powerful engine. It roared to life, then settled down to a low rumble that scared her half to death.

Half an hour later she pulled into her driveway and shut off the engine. She had made it home without putting so much as a scratch on the car's shiny red surface. Not only that, but she hadn't gotten even one speeding ticket. Actually, she hadn't dared to go over twenty miles an hour. There was nothing more humbling than going from a tiny four-cylinder to a jet engine.

DAVID GLANCED at his watch, wondering if his Ferrari was a pile of rubble by now or if Holly was in jail yet. He had argued with himself for a half hour this morning about whether to leave it for her. Somehow his good sense always got lost where she was concerned. He must really be losing it to turn her loose in a car like that.

Maybe she was still asleep. He remembered the way she had looked that morning, curled up in his king-size bed sound asleep. He hadn't wanted to leave her. He knew he should have awakened her before he left, but if he had, he'd still be there.

Now, as he waited with Nick for Patti Bennett, he wondered how he was to survive until he saw Holly again. Damn, he thought, chiding himself for his impatience. The lady was in his blood. Hopefully she would be a part of the rest of his life.

Patti Bennett appeared in the doorway. "Granddad will see you now." She turned her bright smile on Nick. "He's very anxious to meet this famous brother of yours."

Nick grinned at her. "Infamous, you mean."

David stood, giving Patti a smile of his own. "I really appreciate your arranging this, Patti. Are you sure he's up to seeing us?" He had been hesitant about disturbing the elderly man when Nick had told him he was now living in a nursing home. He had celebrated his ninetieth birthday a few weeks ago, but Patti assured David that her grandfather still enjoyed good health and told him not to be surprised if he challenged him to a game of chess. She had also arranged the meeting early in the day because her grandfather tended to tire easily and morning was his best time.

They met with William Montori on a sunny patio at the rear of the sprawling white retirement home. He stood when the three approached, reaching out his hand to grasp David's in a surprisingly strong grip.

"So you're D. W. Branson," he said, his dark eyes alert and piercing. "I can tell you're related to Nick."

David grinned, glancing at his younger brother. "I've been told there's a slight resemblance. Thank you for agreeing to see us, Mr. Montori."

The four of them took seats around a white metal table shaded by a large blue-and-green flowered umbrella. Patti excused herself, explaining that she had arranged for them to have some coffee. She disappeared for a minute, returning with a tray holding a pot of coffee and four cups. She filled the cups and passed one to each person before taking a seat beside Nick.

"Patti tells me you have to tear down that old building," Mr. Montori said. "You know, that was my first project. I'm sorry to hear it won't be around anymore."

David gazed at the elderly gentleman, seeing lingering traces of the man he had once been. There was strength there, and a timeless grace that would never fade. "That's what I would like to talk with you about, Mr. Montori," he said. "I'm not pleased about tearing it down. My original plan was to restore it, but as the restoration work progressed, I realized that building was just too old and had weaknesses I wasn't aware of. When Nick told me you might still have the blueprints, I had the idea of rebuilding it just the way it was built originally."

The other man's eyes gleamed with interest. "Do you think that's possible?"

"I won't know until I see the blueprints."

Montori steepled his fingers and rested his chin on them. "Why is this so important to you?"

David shifted in his chair, aware of three pairs of eyes resting on him. He wrestled with a variety of answers before deciding the truth would be the best. He turned back to Montori. "Because the woman I love will skin me alive and nail my hide to the wall if I touch that building." He saw the humor sparkling in the other man's eyes and grinned. "It would prolong my life considerably if I came up with a workable solution."

Montori laughed heartily, looking at the younger man with respect. "So, it's for a woman, is it?"

David sobered. "Not all of it, sir. It would give me great pleasure to rebuild it just the way it was. I was disappointed to have to stop the renovation."

Montori didn't say anything for the longest time, his thoughts obviously in another place and time. Finally, he nodded. "I'll tell Patti where to find the blueprints and she can deliver them to you in a few days."

"Thank you, sir. And when the building is finished, I'll come and get you and take you on a tour."

"I'd like that, young man."

A loud beeping sounded and David reached into his pocket to quiet the noise. "Is there a telephone around here?" he asked, wondering what emergency had occurred now. Patti directed him to a telephone and he called his office, returning to the table a few minutes later, his eyes dark with anguish.

"Nick, we have to go. A building has collapsed at the civic center."

HOLLY DEBATED taking the Ferrari to work. She stood in the driveway, dressed in a hot-pink suit with a crepe blouse in shades of pink and green, and thought about it. She would clash with the Ferrari, whereas nothing she ever wore clashed with the VW. No matter what she chose, there was sure to be a matching spot somewhere on the small car.

Climbing into the low-slung sports car, Holly told herself that she was doing the right thing. After all, David had been thoughtful enough to make sure she had a way home this morning. The least she could do was deliver the car back to him.

She was still justifying her decision when she turned onto the street where her office building stood. As soon as she arrived she would call David and thank him—and assure him his car had survived. She would also sit down and plan how to tell him that she loved him. A wave of nervousness swept through her, followed by an equally strong wave of determination.

She slammed on the brakes, ignoring the irate drivers behind her. She wouldn't wait. She would tell him now. Somehow she got the car turned around and headed downtown.

It didn't take Holly long to find the Branson Building. It stood out as one of the newest and most imposing in the area. Holly took it as an omen that she had made the right decision when she found a parking place just a few steps away from a side entrance. Within minutes she was in an elevator being whisked to the top floor of the thirty-five-storey edifice. When it stopped with barely a whisper, Holly stepped out onto deep plush carpet and utter bedlam.

She stood for a moment taking in her surroundings with quizzical eyes and a raised brow. People were rushing back and forth, while the receptionist sat with a phone to her ear, writing furiously. Nobody paid the least bit of attention to Holly. She took a few steps forward and, looking past the receptionist's desk to a set of imposing double doors, read the brass nameplate on the wall and knew she had found her destination.

More confident now, Holly stepped eagerly to the door, pausing at the sound of David's familiar voice coming from the other side. His voice was raised to a level Holly had never heard before. He was angry, furious in fact. She hesitated with her hand on the knob.

"I don't care what his excuse is. I want him out and I want him out now! It'll be a cold day in hell before he pours another square foot of cement in this town!"

Holly sucked in her breath, shocked by the venom in David's voice.

"Nobody does this to me and gets away with it!"

The cold deadliness of his voice ripped through her. She found it impossible to move.

"I want him out! Do whatever you have to do, but that man is finished in this town! Understand? Either he goes quietly, or we rip him to shreds. His ass is in a sling and he knows it!"

The blood drained from Holly's face. Her hand tightened on the doorknob, turning her knuckles white with the force.

"No . . . no, I haven't. It's been hectic as hell around here, but I'm on my way down there now. Give that bastard twenty-four hours, max! I'll come after him myself and he'll wish he'd never been born!"

David slammed the phone down and ran his fingers through his hair in an achingly familiar gesture. Holly stared at him, unable for the moment to accept what had just taken place. She had thought that all she had heard about D. W. Branson was wrong, that he wasn't the ruthless, heartless businessman he was purported to be. She had allowed her love—or lust—for him to overshadow her own good sense. How could she have been so blind?

David turned and saw her, swearing softly under his breath as he realized she had overheard part of the conversation.

Holly spun on her heel and ran, brushing past a startled Nick as she tried to put as much distance as she could between herself and the damning scene she had just witnessed. She stepped onto the elevator, hearing David's voice calling her name just as the elevator doors closed behind her.

He didn't swear often, and he wasn't a drinking man, but as the elevator doors closed behind Holly, David thought of all the times in the past few weeks that he had vented his frustration in bad language or had been tempted to drown it in bourbon. All because of one H. C. Nichols. His patience was at an end. He didn't have the time to follow her and explain what had happened. He refused to spend the rest of his life justifying everything he did.

HOLLY SAT at her desk and tried to concentrate on the papers in front of her. Several hours had passed since the fiasco in David's office. She had left the Ferrari parked on a downtown street and taken the bus to her office. Upon arrival, she promptly dropped the car keys in an envelope and sent them back to David by messenger.

An editor of the *CLU Journal*, a national publication for chartered life underwriters, had asked her several weeks ago to write an article. She had agreed but now found it nearly impossible to concentrate. She kept hearing David ordering the destruction of some nameless, faceless man who had dared to cross the infamous D. W. Branson in some way.

"Holly?"

She felt a moment's frustration at the interruption. Hadn't she told Susan she didn't want to be disturbed? Holly lifted her head and inhaled sharply. Nick stood on the other side of her desk. She could tell by the bright light in his eyes, eyes so much like David's, that he was furious.

"What are you doing here?" she demanded, growing uncomfortable under his penetrating stare.

"I'm not sure," he snapped. "I don't know what's going on between you and David, lady, but you don't know him at all, do you?"

Holly stared angrily at him. "I know all I need to know!"

Nick leaned forward to rest his hands on the edge of her desk. "Lady, you don't know anything! If you knew him at all you wouldn't have left him like that this morning. He has enough to deal with. He doesn't need to have to cope with your temper tantrums."

"Temper tantrums! How dare you?" She stood, glaring at Nick. "Get out of here. You don't understand anything."

Nick straightened, taking a deep breath before he spoke. "What you heard this morning, Holly, isn't what you think," he said softly but with a firmness Holly recognized and pegged as a Branson family trait.

"Then what is it?"

"You'll have to ask David."

Why was he here if not to make excuses for his brother's behavior this morning? Holly had no intention of asking David anything. She wanted nothing to do with D. W. Branson or his family.

"I think what I heard was self-explanatory. Now, will you please leave?"

Nick reached into his pocket and withdrew a folded piece of paper, tossing it onto her desk. "You do what you have to do, Holly, but remember this. You're wrong about him. I hope when you finally realize it that it isn't too late." He went to the door, turning with his hand on the knob to say, "If you really care anything for him, turn on the radio. Then you'll know the truth."

Holly sat for a long time after he left, staring at the door, her thoughts in turmoil. David was his brother. Of course Nick would defend him. But why had he bothered to come here at all? Was she wrong again? She had been wrong about so many things concerning D. W. Branson. Could she be wrong about this?

Holly shook her head in denial. No, she knew what she had heard. Nick was just making excuses for his brother.

She reached for the paper Nick had tossed on her desk and slowly unfolded it. It was a map. She knew instinctively that it was a map to David's house. Why would he leave this? Did he expect her to use it? There was a note scrawled across the bottom of the paper. *There's a key in the flowerpot by the back door.*

With great reluctance, Holly reached behind her and turned on the radio.

"...causing one of the buildings at the civic center project to collapse early this morning and injuring several people. Substandard material used by a subcontractor is thought to be the cause of the latest in a series of incidents at the civic center. D. W. Branson, developer of the project, was not available for comment."

Holly covered her face with her hands and let the tears flow.

12

HOLLY PARKED the VW and stared at the rambling frame house, her breath catching in her throat. David lived in the country, and his house was so much like her parents' that she thought she must be dreaming. She got out of the car and looked around at the green pasture-land, thinking that this fit David Winslow Branson far more than the silver-and-chrome condo in town.

The key was right where Nick had said it would be and Holly let herself in the back door, feeling like an intruder as she entered the cool silent kitchen. She stood in a large modern kitchen with warm oak cabinets, blue-and-white-checked wallpaper and red-brick accents. It was a family kitchen and the echoes of that family teased her senses. Curious, Holly left the kitchen to explore the rest of the house, wondering when David would get home.

There was a spacious dining room off the kitchen, with a wide archway leading to a large, high-ceilinged living room. A rock fireplace took up most of one wall. Plush area carpets covered the glistening plank floor while still retaining the warmth and beauty of the wood. The couch was big, cushiony and inviting, covered in a nubby, wheat-colored material. Two chairs in a rich pumpkin color flanked a low table next to the fireplace, and a bar stood against the wall to her left.

Holly moved across the room to a door standing open beneath the stairway. She approached it and looked inside. The room beyond was obviously David's study. A Franklin stove sat in one corner and a worn couch was shoved against another wall. Dominating the room was a large drawing table covered with papers.

She looked around, sensing David's presence in this room. Instinctively she knew he spent a lot of time here. A jacket lay over the arm of the couch and Holly picked it up. It was the same dark blue windbreaker he had worn the night she met him. She lifted it to her face, inhaling the essence of him that lingered in the heavy cotton material.

Her eyes moved to the opposite wall and she stepped closer. The entire Branson clan gazed back at her from over the years. Holly tried to match faces with the names and brief verbal sketches David had given her. Of course she knew Nick. He was a younger, cockier version of David. The one in the air force uniform, taken against a backdrop of rugged mountains and a row of fighter planes, was obviously Gary. Holly found it more difficult to identify Tom and Robert. How could you tell a lawyer from a stockbroker? There were pictures of Cheryl with a good-looking bearded man and two dark-haired children.

The picture of Kate had been taken outside her art gallery in Sante Fe. Even though she had the Branson eyes and dark hair, she was very different from Cheryl. Where Cheryl was sleek and sophisticated, Kate looked like a gypsy. Her unruly dark mane brushed her shoulders, its layered lengths curling even in the dry New

Mexico climate. Holly imagined that in Indianapolis humidity, Kate's hair would border on the unmanageable. Despite their differences, Kate was every bit as beautiful as Cheryl but with a streak of wild recklessness.

Holly left David's study, though she could have spent hours in there. She had the uncomfortable feeling she was invading his privacy, a feeling that prevented her from climbing the stairs to investigate the upper story. Being snoopy was not part of her nature, though her curiosity had gotten her in more trouble than she cared to think about. She went outside, deciding to take a walk around the grounds to help kill time until David came home.

Darkness had fallen before she saw headlights turn into the long driveway and move toward the house. She stood in the living room, clenching and unclenching her hands as she waited, not knowing what his reaction would be. She drew in her breath sharply when he came in, his white shirt streaked with dirt, exhaustion lining his face.

He stopped, staring at her for a long, tense moment before moving to the bar and filling a glass with ice and bourbon. He downed the drink in one gulp, then turned to her, his eyes remote and cool. "What are you doing here, Holly?"

Disconcerted, she clasped her hands together and searched for the right words. "I came here to talk to you."

"Oh, really?" he said, his voice cool and reserved. "After this morning I didn't think you would want anything to do with the scurrilous D. W. Branson."

She flinched. "I was wrong."

"Were you?"

Hot tears stung her eyes. She blinked them back, determined to make him understand that she had been wrong about a lot of things.

He sighed wearily, running his hand through his hair. "I can't do it, Holly," he said evenly. "I can't spend the rest of my life defending every move I make. What you overheard this morning was me making sure that an incompetent contractor wouldn't have another chance to hurt someone. What happens the next time someone like that almost costs me the lives of three of my best men? My foreman, a man who's been with me from the beginning, is lying in the hospital tonight because of that greedy bastard! What was I supposed to do, let him go on until he kills someone? He came as close today as I ever want to see."

She took a step toward him. "David, I love you."

He gave a short derisive laugh. "Well, you know something, Holly? A few hours ago I would have given my life to hear you say those words, but..." He paused, then looked at her in that steady, direct way he had. "Sometimes love just isn't enough."

Holly went to him, determined not to let the most important thing in her life slip away. She reached up and spread her fingers across his cheek. "You're right, you know. There are times when love isn't enough, when you have to reevaluate the issues and sort out what is truth and what is garbage. Sometimes you have to go by instinct, by what you feel inside. I think it's called gut instinct. It's also called trust." She saw the wariness in his eyes, but she also saw the love he couldn't quite hide, no matter how he tried. There was one way that might make him believe her. "I love you, Mr. D. W. Branson Development, Incorporated."

He held his breath for a moment, wanting to believe her. It seemed that his very life depended on it. "Holly, do you know that's the first time you've said my name without scorn?"

She put her fingers to his lips. "Don't let it go to your head, Branson." Her eyes darkened. "I was coming to your office this morning to tell you that it didn't matter anymore, that I loved you no matter what name you carried. I—" Before she could say anything more she was in his arms.

He held her close, feeling all the scattered pieces of his life coming together in this woman. "Lord, Holly, this has been one of the worst days of my life. I thought I'd lost you. I nearly lost Jake. When I was driving home, I had the feeling that nothing mattered anymore, that there was nothing left for me to hang on to."

She smiled up at him through her tears. When she thought about how close she had come to losing him, a cold chill went through her. "That's over, David. It's all behind us."

He laughed shakily. "Yes, it is over, isn't it." He looked down at his shirt. "I could use a shower." He pulled Holly against him. "Stay with me tonight, Holly. I don't think I could stand it without you here."

She wrapped her arms around him and laid her head on his chest, listening to the steady beat of his heart. "You'd have a hard time getting rid of me, Branson." She was quiet for a while, holding him close, feeling his strength. "You aren't to blame for what happened today, David." She knew it would take time for him to accept that. She was determined to be there with him, to help him over every rough spot he would ever encounter. Finally she stepped back and looked up at him with a smile. "How about that shower?"

He gave her one of his slow enticing smiles. "Are you volunteering to wash my back?"

"Yes, and anything else that needs my undivided attention."

He sucked in his breath, his eyes darkening with desire. "You are a wanton, Holly Nichols."

"Yep, and you have only yourself to blame."

He released her and stepped away, frowning. "I have to call the hospital and check on Jake."

"Of course." She watched him dial the phone, saw the deep lines of worry around his eyes and mouth. Would it ever cease to amaze her, this caring for other people that was an intrinsic part of D. W. Branson?

He hung up the phone and came to stand beside her. "The hospital says Jake is going to be okay, that he regained consciousness about an hour ago."

"David, I'm so glad."

He lowered his head and took her lips in a long, seductive, thoroughly passionate kiss that left her breathless. When he finally released her she felt as limp as a rag doll.

"Last one in the shower has to fix dinner." He was halfway across the room and in the process of stripping off his shirt by the time the words were out of his mouth.

Holly came out of her trance. "You cheated!" she yelped, taking off after him. He reached the shower two steps ahead of her. She stood outside the frosted door with her hands on her hips, still dressed in her bra and panty hose. "No fair, Branson! I had twice as many clothes as you." The only reply she got was the sound of rushing water. She stripped off her panty hose and bra and slid the door open.

David grasped her by the waist and hauled her into the shower. "It took you long enough, Nichols."

"Keep it up and you can cook your own dinner."

He reached for the soap and sudsed both his hands, then put the bar back in the dish and reached out to touch her.

"I should be doing this to you," she said softly, closing her eyes and giving in to the wonderful sensations flooding her as David's work-roughened hands began smoothing the soap over her water-slick body.

David looked down at her, his stomach churning at the thought of how close he had come to losing her.

Holly felt his hand tremble and she opened her eyes to look up at him. Remnants of fear lingered in his eyes and she reached up to touch his face. "David," she whispered, "everything is going to be all right now." Warm water streamed over them as her hand slid to the back of his head and she raised herself up to taste his slightly parted lips. There was something uniquely erotic about being trapped within the confines of the shower stall, feeling the beat of the water on her back and the beat of David's heart against her breasts. The heat of his mouth matched the heat of the pulsating water and Holly felt herself melting against him.

"Holly, Holly," he whispered in a husky, slightly tremulous cadence. He kissed her lips, her cheek, the tip of her nose, the arch of her eyebrow. His arms went around her, drawing her close, though even when the full length of her was pressed against him, he longed to bring her closer still. "I almost lost you, Holly," he murmured in her ear. "I wouldn't want to go on living without you. I love you so."

Holly placed a hand on each side of his head and gazed into his tortured eyes. "You would survive without me. Look at all you've survived in the past."

"But I wouldn't like it." He bent his head to take her lips in a kiss she was sure raised the steam level in the bathroom a few notches. "I need you, Holly. Now," he whispered raggedly. The hard evidence of his arousal pressed against her. How quickly she could stir a fire in his blood. He reached behind her and shut off the water, then slid the glass door open and, lifting her up in his arms, stepped out into the steamy bathroom.

He released her and she stood, watching him through passion-glazed eyes as he took a thick blue towel off the bar on the shower door and began to slowly wipe the moisture from her body.

"David," she managed to say, feeling the familiar heat rising in her. Almost in a daze, she took the towel from him and began to rub it over his lean body. She couldn't get enough of touching him. She toweled his muscular arms, his broad chest, then moved the towel lower to blot the water from his flat stomach. Then she moved still lower.

David inhaled sharply, reaching out to grasp Holly's shoulders and lift her against him. "Enough," he muttered, taking the towel from her and tossing it toward the hamper behind him. He took her in his arms and lowered his mouth to hers.

It wasn't enough. Not nearly enough. Lifting her in his arms once again, David carried her from the bathroom to his bed and laid her gently on the quilted comforter.

Her love for him shining in her eyes, Holly looked at him. She raised her arms and he went to her with a low moan. Only in her arms could he find the peace he so sorely needed. The realization that she truly belonged to him slowly began to sink in.

She felt the tremor that racked his body and understood. With a woman's intuition, she sensed his need for her. She placed her hands on his chest and gently pushed until he lay on his back.

She knelt beside him looking at him with a wealth of love reflected in her eyes. The hand she placed on his chest trembled slightly. She bent to kiss him softly, carefully.

"I never knew it could be like this," she murmured. "So much joy. So much sharing." She indulged herself, flicking out her tongue to lap at a pearl-sized droplet of water clinging to his chin. "I love touching you." Her hand moved slowly across his chest and down his side, coming to rest on the indentation of his waist.

"Holly." His voice was a low agonized whisper. Would it ever fade, this sense of wonder and completeness? He thought back to the moment this morning when he'd hung up the phone and looked up to see her standing in the doorway, an expression of horror and disbelief on her face. He had nearly lost her twice. He couldn't bear it if he lost her forever. The utter bleakness of life without her made him cringe. It had been bad enough in increments of days and hours. He knew his life would lose all meaning without her in it.

Holly settled herself along the length of him, draping one leg over his. Breasts pressed against his chest, she nibbled at the lobe of his ear. "Tell me what you want, David," she whispered.

He wrapped his arms around her and lifted her to lie full-length atop him. "I want all of you," he murmured, running his hand into the valley of her spine.

Holly found his lips in a kiss that soon flamed wildly. She had wanted to love him slowly, thoroughly. She hadn't meant for this to get so out of control. David lifted her to give him access to her breasts. Holly threw back her head and closed her eyes, reveling in the feel of his hot wet mouth on her sensitive skin. She was fully, vitally aware of every inch of his skin that touched hers.

Finally, when she could bear it no longer, she straddled him, taking him inside her with a soft cry of fulfillment. She looked down at his face, at his heavy-lidded eyes, which smoldered with green fire, loving the low sounds of pleasure that whispered from his lips as she began to move. He clutched at her hips, thrusting still deeper inside her. Her slender control snapped and she loved him with a wildness that left them both exhausted and slick with perspiration when it was over.

Their coming together was a celebration of life, of love. Their joy in each other knew no bounds.

Holly felt content to lie in his arms afterward, to know he would be there every day for the rest of her life.

"Where did you go so early this morning?"

"I had an appointment."

Holly lifted her head to gaze down at him, noting a strangely satisfied gleam in his eyes. "Who with? A rooster?"

David chuckled. "I don't think William Montori would appreciate being called a rooster." He hugged her, then briefly told her about the meeting.

She stared at him, wondering at the lengths he would go to please her. "Will it work? Do you think you can do it?"

He didn't meet her eyes. "If I don't, are you still going to sue me?"

Holly gasped, then saw the teasing light in his eyes. She shook her head, content to have his arm around her and his lips gently caressing hers. He took her hand and lifted it to his lips, kissing each fingertip in turn.

A HALF HOUR LATER, dressed in one of David's long-sleeved flannel shirts, Holly stood at the counter in the kitchen tossing salad for dinner. David had lighted the grill and defrosted two steaks in the microwave. He came to stand beside her.

"Where's Nick? Isn't he staying with you?"

He dropped a kiss on her slightly parted lips. "He's at the condo." He kissed her more firmly. "There's one thing I can think of that will make this night perfect."

She slapped his hand as he tried to swipe a radish from the salad bowl. "And just what would that be, Mr. Branson?"

David held a beautiful and very familiar sapphire ring up, then reached for her hand and slipped it on her finger. "For you to tell me you'll become Mrs. Branson," he said huskily.

"Cheryl won't like your giving her ring away."

"It isn't Cheryl's. It belonged to my mother."

"David . . ."

"Say yes, Holly."

Holly felt her breath catch in her throat. She fluttered her eyelashes at him. "Why, Mistuh Branson, suh, ah haven't known ya'll for very long."

David grasped her by the shoulders and turned her to face him. "Say yes, Holly," he growled.

"Well, I never did tell Michael our engagement was a joke."

He shook her gently. "Say yes!"

"The Indy 500 is next week—"

"Holly!" he muttered in frustration. "I'll fly your whole family here and we'll rent the racetrack for the reception."

Holly draped her arms around his neck, plunging her fingers into the soft thickness of his hair. "I haven't said yes yet."

"Say it," he whispered, kissing the corner of her mouth.

"Yes."

Lynda Ward's TOUCH THE STARS

... the final book in the *The Welles Family Trilogy*

Lynda Ward's TOUCH THE STARS ... the final book in the Welles Family Trilogy. All her life Kate Welles Brock has sought to win the approval of her wealthy and powerful father, even going as far as to marry Burton Welles's handpicked successor to the Corminco Corporation.

Now, with her marriage in tatters behind her, Kate is getting the first taste of what it feels like to really live. Her glorious romance with the elusive Paul Florian is opening up a whole new world to her.... Kate is as determined to win the love of her man as she is to prove to her father that she is the logical choice to succeed him as head of Corminco....

Don't miss TOUCH THE STARS, a Harlequin Superromance coming to you in September.

If you missed the first two books of this exciting trilogy, #317 RACE THE SUN and #321 LEAP THE MOON, and would like to order them, send your name, address and zip or postal code, along with a check or money order for $2.95 for each book ordered (plus $1.00 postage and handling) payable to Harlequin Reader Service to:

In the U.S.	In Canada
901 Fuhrmann Blvd.	P.O. Box 609
Box 1396	Ft. Erie, Ontario
Buffalo, NY 14240-9954	L2A 5X3

LYNDA-1C

ABANDON YOURSELF TO

Temptation ™

In September's Harlequin Temptation books you'll get more than just terrific sexy romance—you'll get $2 worth of **Jovan Musk** fragrance coupons **plus** an opportunity to get a very special, unique nightshirt.

Harlequin's most sensual series will also be featuring four of Temptation's favourite authors writing the Montclair Emeralds quartet.

Harlequin Temptation in September— too hot to miss!

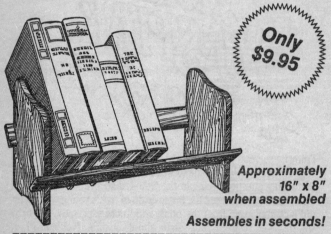

HARLEQUIN SIGNATURE EDITION

VIOLET WINSPEAR

HOUSE OF STORMS

Editorial secretary Debra Hartway travels to the Salvador family's rugged Cornish island home to work on Jack Salvador's latest book. Disturbing questions hang in the troubled air over Lovelis Island. What or who had caused the tragic death of Jack's young wife? Why did Jack stay away from the home and, more especially, the baby son he loved so well? And—why should Rodare, Jack's brother, who had proved himself a man of the highest integrity, constantly invade Debra's thoughts with such passionate, dark desires...?

Violet Winspear, who has written more than 65 romance novels translated worldwide into 18 languages, is one of Harlequin's best-loved and bestselling authors. HOUSE OF STORMS, her second title in the Harlequin Signature Edition program, is a full-length novel rich in romantic tradition and intriguingly spiced with an atmosphere of danger and mystery.

Watch for HOUSE OF STORMS—coming in October!   HOFS-1